"Why are eyes m... in a rush of helpless confusion.

"Why am I so bitter…?" he mused. His voice was lazy and thoughtful, but his dark eyes were coldly hostile and a shiver of dread slithered down Laura's spine. "Why do *you* think I'm bitter?"

"Because your pride was dented when…" Her voice faltered.

"Say it, Laura," he commanded silkily. "After all, it has been a long time since we last set eyes on one another. What could be more natural than to go over old ground?"

"What's the point of all this? Do you have any intention of buying the stables, Gabriel, or did you decide to get me here so that you could watch me squirm? Humiliate me because I once turned down your proposal of marriage?"

There. It was out, and they stared at one another in lengthening silence.

RED HOT REVENGE

The Millionaire's Revenge
by
Cathy Williams

There are times in a man's life…

when only seduction will settle old scores!

Pick up our exciting new series of revenge-themed
romances—they're recommended and red-hot!

Cathy Williams

THE MILLIONAIRE'S REVENGE

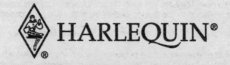

RED HOT REVENGE

HARLEQUIN®

TORONTO • NEW YORK • LONDON
AMSTERDAM • PARIS • SYDNEY • HAMBURG
STOCKHOLM • ATHENS • TOKYO • MILAN • MADRID
PRAGUE • WARSAW • BUDAPEST • AUCKLAND

ISBN 0-373-12299-3

THE MILLIONAIRE'S REVENGE

First North American Publication 2003.

Copyright © 2002 by Cathy Williams.

This edition published by arrangement with Harlequin Books S.A.

® and TM are trademarks of the publisher. Trademarks indicated with
® are registered in the United States Patent and Trademark Office, the
Canadian Trade Marks Office and in other countries.

Visit us at www.eHarlequin.com

Printed in U.S.A.

CHAPTER ONE

GABRIEL GREPPI stood outside the compact, ivy-clad Victorian house for a few minutes, his hands thrust into the pockets of his beaten suede jacket. He glanced up towards the left of the house, and saw that her room was in darkness. It would be. She would be at the stables now, even though it was after nine and the countryside was sunk in the frozen grip of winter.

The thought of her brought a smile to his lips. For her, he would go through this, but it wouldn't always be this way. He knew it. Could feel it in his bones. Knocking on the door of this house and being made to feel like a beggar, a distasteful presence to be endured by her parents with that particularly freezing politeness so typical of the British upper crust. No, things would change. He was only twenty-two and it might be a long haul, but things would change.

He hardened his jaw and pressed his finger to the doorbell, listening to it resound through the house, then he lounged against the doorframe and waited until the door was cautiously pulled open. Gabriel was tempted to ask whether they were expecting bandits to ring the bell before entering the house, but he refrained. A keen sense of humour had never been one of Peter Jackson's striking qualities, although that might just have been towards him.

'Greppi. What brings you here, boy?'

Gabriel gritted his teeth together and summoned up all his self-control not to respond with something he would live to regret.

'Could I have a word with you, Mr Jackson?' He insinuated his foot through the small opening, just in case Peter Jackson gave in to the temptation to slam the door in his face.

'What, now? Can't it wait?'

Peter Jackson gave an impatient click of his tongue and regarded Gabriel's dark, handsome face with irritation, then he reluctantly pulled open the door and stepped back. 'If you've come to see my daughter, then you can start heading back to that house of yours, boy. Laura's in bed and I have no intention of getting her out of it at this ungodly hour.'

'It's nine o'clock.'

'Precisely.'

'And I haven't come to see Laura, I have come to see you. You and your wife.' Gabriel fought to maintain his composure but, under his weathered jacket and faded jeans, every muscle in his hard body had tensed.

That stopped Peter Jackson in his tracks. He paused and narrowed his blue eyes. 'I hope you don't intend to ask any favours of me, boy, because I can tell you right now that the answer is a resounding negative. I am not in the habit of bailing out anyone financially.'

'I have not come here to ask for money.' He kept his tone as polite as he could, but the derision underneath was unmistakable and the older man's mouth tightened.

'Then say what you have to say and leave.'

This was turning out to be a big mistake. He had chosen to take the honourable path and now he wondered what had possessed him.

'Perhaps I could speak with your wife as well.'

'Oh, very well. But you'll have to be brief. My wife is not a well woman. She needs to get to bed at a reasonable hour.' He turned and began walking towards the snug and

Gabriel followed behind him, slightly taller and with the easy, graceful stride of someone attuned with his body.

'Lizzie, darling, we have an unexpected visitor. No, no need to get up. It's just Greppi.'

Elizabeth Jackson sat in one of the big, padded armchairs, a fragile figure but with the stunning prettiness of a woman who even now, in her mid-fifties, could still make heads turn. The classic English rose who exuded good breeding from every one of her fingertips. Neither invited him to sit, nor was he offered a drink, although both were, he could tell, curious to find out what the hell he was doing in their house at the unseemly hour of nine in the evening.

Peter Jackson stood behind his wife's chair, as ruggedly impressive as she was delicately pretty. 'If you're thinking of buying one of the horses, Greppi, then you're out of luck. Laura tells me that you have a knack with Barnabus, but he's not for sale. If you could afford him, which I frankly doubt. Might be a bit tempestuous, that stallion, but he'll make a damned fine racehorse with the proper training, so don't think you can cut yourself a deal cheaply simply because you know how to handle him. Or, for that matter, because my daughter chooses to associate with you. I am doing enough of a good deed by employing you to do odd jobs around the stables on the weekends.'

'I have come to ask for your daughter's hand in marriage.'

I have come to tell you that I am from another planet. I have come to tell you that I am the son of Satan. Gabriel watched their astounded expressions and figured that he might as well have confronted them with either of those two possibilities.

'I know that Laura thinks the world of you both and I would very much like to receive your blessing.' Gabriel's nerves remained steady as he stared at them both. Young he might be in years, but his life had not been an easy ride and he had learned to deal with pretty much anything that could be thrown at him. Including Laura's snobbish, insular parents who had made it clear from the very first moment they had set eyes on him that he was one of life's more lowly inhabitants.

'I love your daughter, and whilst I realise that at the moment I may not have much to offer her, I assure—'

That broke the gaping silence surrounding them. The mention of his penury. Peter Jackson flung back his head and roared with laughter, then he sobered up sufficiently to wipe a few residual tears of mirth from his eyes.

'What, are you completely mad, Greppi? Now you listen to me and you listen carefully, boy.' The older man leaned over his wife and enunciated his words very slowly, as if addressing someone whose grasp of English was faulty. 'Neither Lizzie nor myself approved of your *involvement* with Laura, but she's a big girl and there has not been much we could do about it. However, the only way you will marry our daughter is over my dead body! Do you read me loud and clear, boy? She is our jewel and there is no way on the face of this green earth that we will give our blessing to any marriage between the two of you.'

'She's only a child, Gabriel.' Elizabeth Jackson's voice was quiet but firm. 'Nineteen years old. And you're only a child as well.'

'Why don't we cut through the *child* argument and get to the heart of the matter?' Gabriel said with rigid self-control. 'You see me as an inferior citizen because I am not British.'

'That's not true, young man!' But Elizabeth Jackson's protest was as empty as a shell. The truth was stamped on her husband's face and Gabriel turned his head to one side in anger.

'You're not what we have in mind for a son-in-law, Greppi. I have no doubt that you'll make something of yourself, and good luck to you, but Laura deserves...'

'Better?' Gabriel's voice was spiked with acidity.

'Call it what you will. And I warn you, Greppi, you leave our daughter alone. We haven't wanted to interfere, but you are no longer welcome at these stables. You can find somewhere else to do your riding and earn your extra money.'

And that was the end of the discussion. Gabriel could see it in the way the old man turned towards the window, offering him the dismissive view of his back.

'Very well.' Jet-black eyes smouldered as he looked at the two of them who would both breathe a sigh of heartfelt relief when he disappeared out of their line of vision.

But this was not over. He had appealed to them for their blessing and they had turned him down. Laura would not. He would have preferred to have married the woman he loved with her parents fully on his side, but if that was not to be the case, then so be it.

He turned on his heel and walked out of the room, letting himself out of the front door. The meeting, which he had imagined would have lasted at least an hour, an hour of persuading them that, whatever their prejudices, he would devote his entire life to making their beloved daughter happy, had lasted a scant ten minutes.

The stables were set away from the house. Gabriel made sure to exit along the drive, knowing that her father would probably have leapt to the window just to make sure that he was leaving the premises, and, after a few minutes of walking through the cutting night air, he abruptly turned to his right and ploughed his way back towards the extensive stables.

He had arranged to meet her there and she would be waiting for him. The thought of that quelled some of the fire burning in his soul and he relaxed his pace, filling his head with images of her.

The stables stretched around a huge courtyard, which was occasionally used for lessons for beginners. A long, sheltered corridor bordered the sprawling sweep of the individual horses' quarters and Gabriel swiftly and assuredly made his way towards Barnabus's stall.

The light was on and she was grooming him, her long fingers stroking the mane, running along the proud length of his head.

Gabriel felt the familiar hot stirring in his loins and drew his breath in sharply, and both Laura and horse turned to look at him.

'I didn't expect you so early,' she murmured, leaving the horse and wiping her hands along her jeans. She smiled and lifted her face to his, giving a soft purr of contentment as his mouth brushed hers.

'Disappointed?'

'Hardly!'

'Do you want me to give you a hand here?'

'Oh, no. There's nothing to be done. I was just chatting to Barnabus.'

'About me, I hope,' Gabriel murmured softly, pulling her towards him and keeping her there, with his hands on her rear, so that she could feel exactly what she did to him.

She was the perfect combination of her parents. She had the height of her father and the blonde beauty of her mother. When she tilted her head back, as she was doing now, her waist-length hair rippled over his hands like strands of silk. White silk.

'But of course,' she agreed with a small laugh of delight. 'Who else? What have you been doing since I last saw you? Have you missed me?'

I've been slaving at an incompetently run engineering company. I've been poring over books so that I don't completely lose track of my Economics degree. I've been putting aside every sweat-earned penny so that I can afford to eat when I return to university. Oh, yes, and I've asked your father for your hand in marriage and it was bitten off.

That little titbit, he decided, he would keep to himself. Now, he would lose himself in her and then he would propose. Her parents would simply have to accept him because they would have no choice.

'If you're finished with Barnabus...' he murmured, tucking her hair behind her ear and nibbling it with his teeth until she squirmed.

'The office...?'

'Out here, if you'd prefer, although I cannot truthfully say that I would welcome dealing with the frostbite afterwards...'

The office comprised three rooms attached to the far end of the stables. One small sitting area for clients, a room in which the books were kept and a bathroom, all furnished with exquisite taste. Soon, Gabriel thought, they would no longer need to scurry and hide and make love like thieves in the night. He imagined her face as she heard him ask her to marry him and he felt a fierce quiver of possessiveness.

'What's the matter?'

He turned to see that she was staring up at him, all wide-eyed and concerned, and he smiled.

'Do you ever dream of us making love in a proper bed?' he asked softly, unlocking the door to the office with the

12 THE MILLIONAIRE'S REVENGE

key that, unimaginatively, was hidden under one of the plant pots outside. He pushed open the door and then closed it behind them, capturing her against the back of the door and kissing the nape of her neck. 'A proper, king-sized bed complete with satin sheets and a feather duvet?'

'A cramped single bed would do,' Laura murmured, sighing as his tongue trailed along her neck. 'Anywhere but here. I have nightmares about Dad bursting in when we're in the middle of…of…'

'Making love…?' he finished smoothly for her and she coiled against him with a smile. His voice always did this to her, turned her legs to water. His dark, deep voice with the lingering traces of his Argentinian background, and his smoky, sexy eyes that could stroke her body even when he wasn't touching her.

He had turned up out of the blue one wintry morning a year ago. One minute she had been bending over, grooming one of the horses, her long hair roughly braided back away from her face, and she had stood up to find him staring at her from the stable door, his hands in his pockets, his body leaning against the rough doorframe. He had heard about their stables and he had come to see whether he could earn some money helping out because he loved horses and was a natural at handling them. He had only just come up there to live. His father had been made redundant from his post as a teacher and, whilst he could cope until he located another job, there simply was no longer enough to cover his son's university fees. Gabriel needed to work for a year and had taken a job nearby at a small company, interrupting his university career until he could accumulate sufficient money to put himself through the remainder of his course. He had explained all of this without taking his eyes off her and without moving from his indolent stance by the door. Laura had listened and had hardly heard a word he had been saying. She had been too overwhelmed by his sheer animal beauty.

'Are you suggesting that you want to make love to me?' Gabriel whispered in her ear now, and Laura made a low, gurgling sound as he cupped her face in his hands and began kissing her jawbone with infinite, lingering tenderness. Underneath her three layers of clothing, she could already feel her breasts aching to be touched.

It was dark in the office. Dark but warm, with the small fan heater gently purring like a soothing background noise.

'What would you do if I said that I just wasn't in the mood?' Laura teased, curling her fingers into his dark hair and nudging his face up so that she could cover his mouth with hers. The kiss was fiercely passionate, tongue pressing against tongue with an urgency that spoke volumes about the four days during which they had not seen one another. An eternity, it seemed to her.

'I would call you a liar,' he teased back. He slipped his hands beneath her thick, woollen jumper and hooked his fingers under the waistband of her jeans, then he gently circled his fingers round so that he could undo the button and slide down the zip, whilst Laura made a tiny moaning sound in anticipation of what was to come. Heaven on earth. It was the only way she could describe it. Sometimes when, for whatever reason, they had not managed to touch one another for a while, they would scrabble to make love, ripping each other's clothes off in their eagerness to unite their bodies.

Tonight, Gabriel thought, was a special night. Tonight, they would take their time.

He led her towards the back of the office, where a long sofa was ranged against the wall. In the beginning, it had felt odd to make love in the place where Peter Jackson's accountant did the books. Necessity, however, was the mother of invention, and over time the oddness had faded away.

The sofa could have been specially designed for coupling. Laura had once laughingly told him that, in her opinion, Phillip Carr had stationed it there so that when he came twice a week to do the accounts he had somewhere to nod off when the boredom of the numbers began to get to him.

'Let me look at you,' Laura said huskily, stretching her long body on the sofa and staring up at him as he towered over her. 'You know I love looking at you get undressed.' She loosely clasped her arms above her head so that a slither of flat, pale stomach was visible.

'I have no idea why.' He gave a low, teasing laugh.

'And who's the liar now? You know exactly why I love looking at you. You have the most beautiful body I have ever set eyes on in my life. You're as powerful and muscular as any one of our prized racehorses.'

'Thank you very much,' he said drily, although he knew that, coming from her, this was the biggest compliment she could give him.

He shrugged off his bomber jacket, then tugged his thick jumper over his head, followed by his tee shirt, once black, now faded to a dark, uneven grey.

Laura gave an involuntary groan of physical response at his bare-backed torso, just a shadowy outline in the darkness. She had seen him bare-backed before, though. In the summer, when he had stripped off his shirt and ridden Barnabus, without her father's knowledge. Her memory could easily fill in the details of how he'd looked, his body bronzed, his muscles defined and rippling with every little movement. She watched, heavy-eyed, as he removed his trousers and the boxer shorts that were low slung on his waist, and her smile met his.

'Enjoying the view?'

Laura sighed with delicious assent and stood up, ready to wriggle out of her jeans. Her body was on fire. Just looking at him was enough to make her breathing shallow and unsteady.

'Allow me, *querida*,' he murmured. It was one of the rare times when he uttered an endearment. He was a man of passion but essentially a controlled man. Outbursts of verbal emotion were not in his nature. No phoney declarations of love for him. Laura appreciated him for that. His tenderness went beyond mundane utterances. Which was why his endearment now made her heart flutter with pleasure. She allowed him to strip off her jumper, her long-sleeved rugby shirt, which had been a legacy from her father's barnstorming days when he'd played rugby for the county, her tee shirt, leaving only her lacy bra, which barely covered the full swell of her generous breasts.

'Beautiful. You are exquisite.' He dipped his finger into the hollow between her breasts and languidly stroked her, mesmerising her with his eyes until her breath caught in her throat. 'I will never tire of looking at you, touching you.'

Laura laughed softly and caught his finger in her hand, raising it to her mouth so that she could draw it in between her lips, whilst she continued to look at him with her amazing chocolate-brown eyes. With her other hand, she lightly traced the hard muscles of his flattened stomach, down to where his manhood was sheathed with dark, vibrant hair.

'What, *never*? Even when you go to university in September to finish your course? And all those young, beautiful girls are there making eyes and flinging themselves at you?'

'Would you be jealous?' He slipped his hands down her waist and began easing her jeans off, tucking the tips of his fingers into her briefs as she wriggled out of the jeans and gently kicked them to one side.

'Oh, absolutely, Gabriel. Which is why I don't think about it.' She licked his mouth with her tongue and pushed her body against his. She was only a few inches shorter than he was and their bodies made a perfect match, fitting against each other as though specifically designed for the purpose. 'I prefer to concentrate on the here and now.' To prove her point, she drew his hands down to the front of her briefs, wantonly offering him the temptation to explore the honeyed, womanly centre wetly waiting for his expert touch.

'You're a witch, Laura.' Gabriel tugged down her underwear and then unclasped her bra, allowing her full breasts with their rosy peaked nipples to spill forth in all their bountiful glory.

'Only since I met you.' And they both knew that that was true. She had come to him as a virgin, driven into his arms by a force of attraction she had never in her life experienced before. The many boys she had laughingly dated in the past had faded into insignificance alongside the potent, raven-haired stranger who had walked into her life and taken it over.

'Right answer.' He cupped her breasts with his hands. God, he had meant for this to go oh, so slowly, but with her naked body pressing against his he had to fight to maintain control. When she rubbed against him as she was doing now, he just wanted to take her, to feel her body joined to his in heated, pulsating fulfilment.

He guided her back to the sofa, but when she made to lie down he urged her back up, sitting, so that he could part her legs and kneel between them. The perfect position in which to devote his attention to her perfect breasts. He nuzzled them as Laura flung back her head and made no effort to silence her groans of exquisite pleasure. His tongue played with the tips of her nipples and then his mouth circled first one, then the other, pulling and sucking until she began to buck gently against him with her hands firmly clasped in his hair.

No other man would ever touch her like this. She was his, he thought with a surge of possessive elation.

He placed the flat of his hands against the soft inner flesh of her thighs and, whilst she was still reeling from the effects of his mouth on her sensitised breasts, he began a more intimate exploration that had her writhing and gasping as his tongue found the protruding nub of her femininity.

In between her panting, he could hear the abandoned rawness of her voice as she verbalised her passion and that was a powerful aphrodisiac. With a final flick of his tongue deep into the moist sweetness, he rose up and thrust into her, moving strong and deep until their bodies reached the peak of mutual fulfilment.

Only when they were physically spent did he shift her lengthways onto the sofa so that he could lie beside her. A tight fit but it felt so right with his leg draped over her body.

'Wouldn't it be wonderful if we could actually fall asleep together, Gabriel? Like this? Spend the night together?' Laura cradled his head against her breasts and smiled down at him. She swept some of her tangled hair away from her face and continued to watch him as he idly coiled one long, stray tendril around his finger. He held the hair between his fingers and languorously dangled it over her nipple until she giggled.

'I could come and visit you when you're at university,' she carried on dreamily. 'Your own room. Bliss. Or else you could come and visit me at university. Taking this year off's been good, but I can't wait to stretch my wings and leave home.'

'Edinburgh is a long way to commute from London.' He touched her nipple with the pad of his thumb and felt her body still under his touch.

'What are you saying to me, Gabriel?' Laura jerked his head up so that their eyes met in the semi-darkness. 'Too far to commute? I know it won't be like it is now, with you working locally, but we'll still see each other, won't we? Fate brought us together. I know that. Why else would you have happened to see that advert for a job all the way up here, with lodgings provided? And why else would you have found your way here, at these stables, to earn some extra money, meeting me in the process? Fate.'

'Ah, but are you sure you will have time for me?' he teased. 'Studying to become a vet is not going to leave you much time for entertaining old…acquaintances…'

Laura caught the wicked gleam in his eyes and breathed a silent sigh of relief.

'So it's just as well that you're not an old acquaintance, isn't it?' She allowed herself a little laugh and relaxed back against the sofa.

'There *is* another solution, of course, to the problem of meeting up regularly…'

'Oh, yes. What's that?' She ran one foot along the length of his thigh. 'Have you suddenly discovered a vast sum of money somewhere and bought a helicopter so you can fly up to see me every evening?'

'Laura, will you marry me?'

It took a few seconds for Laura's drowsy brain to absorb what he had just said. 'You're joking, aren't you?'

'I have never been more serious about anything in my life, *querida*.'

Laura shifted herself into a sitting position and drew her

legs up. She desperately wanted to switch the light on so that she could see the expression on his face, but switching on lights was totally out of the question. The office block was not at all visible from the house, but it was still a chance they never took. Instead, she peered at him.

'Marry you, Gabriel?' He was deadly serious. His body language conveyed as much.

'Of course, it would be a bit difficult to start with, but we could find somewhere cheap to rent in London and as soon as we are settled you could re-apply to a London university to do your course. Having to come up here to work and save money has slowed me down a bit, but I have only one year left to complete and then I will be earning money. We won't go hungry, *mi amor*, of that you can be certain.'

'Gabriel...' Her voice was a low stammer as the implications of marrying him slammed into her like a fist. Her parents would die. Her mother certainly would. She knew that they had viewed her relationship with Gabriel with growing unease, and they probably weren't even aware that they were lovers. Her mother had shown slightly more fortitude than her father and had contented herself with the occasional observations that she should be careful not to become too emotionally entangled. Her father had been more outspoken. He had told her only two weeks ago in no uncertain terms that he disapproved strongly of what was going on and that he wanted her to end any relationship before it got out of control.

She could feel him pulling away from her and she reached out and gripped his hand tightly. 'God, Gabriel, I love you so much. I've never felt anything like this before. You know that. I've told you that a thousand times. More. But...'

'But...?' No, this was not going how he'd imagined, not

at all. He had expected her immediate, glowing accep-
tance. Yes, there would be one or two problems, but nothing that could not be handled. Nothing that they could not
discuss and solve. His pride began shifting into place. He
could feel it closing around him like a vice and he took a
few deep breaths to steady himself.

'I'm only nineteen,' she said, half pleading. 'Can't we
just…carry on like this…?'

'You mean sneaking around your parents' backs because you're ashamed to be seen openly with me?' he
accused harshly, and Laura flinched back from the tone of
his voice.

'That's unfair!'

'Is it?' He stood up and began putting on his boxer
shorts, his jeans whilst she continued to watch him with a
growing sense of panic. 'It seems to me, Laura, that you
don't object to my presence in your bed, or should I say
on this cursed sofa, but you object to it everywhere else
in your life!' Rage had now settled firmly into place. He
remembered her father's burst of laughter at the unimag-
inable idea that a poor Argentinian might want to marry
his daughter and wondered whether it was so far removed
from her own refusal. Because refuse she had. No point
trying to cover it up in pretty packaging. She had turned
him down.

'Stop it, Gabriel!' She sprang to her feet, shaking with
dismay, and tried to get his hands between hers, but he
brushed them aside and carried on getting dressed whilst
she stood before him in all her naked splendour. Her vulnerability only occurred to her when he had slung his tee
shirt over him, and then she hurriedly began to follow suit,
flinging on her clothes with shaking hands.

'God, you even still wear your father's clothes!'

'He doesn't *wear* this! And I only put it on because it's

warm and it was the first thing that came to hand when I left the house tonight! Left the house *to meet you!*'

'Yes, under cover of darkness! Would you have been so desperate to come rushing out if I had invited you to dine with me? If you had been forced to tell *Mummy and Daddy* that you were going on a date with me?'

'Yes, I would have been just as desperate!' Her eyes glittered with unshed tears, which she swallowed back. 'But when have you ever asked me out on a date?' she flung at him. 'You come and work and sometimes we ride off together away from the house and we sleep together, but when have you *ever* asked me to go out to dinner with you?'

'You know the situation!' His voice cut through her like a knife and sent a shiver of despair fluttering down her spine. 'I have always made it clear that every meagre penny I get from the company is ploughed back into my bank account so that I can support myself financially for my last year at university!'

'*I've* offered to pay!'

'Accept money from a woman? Never.'

'Because you're so damned proud! And you're letting your pride destroy what we have now!'

'What we have? We have nothing.'

The silence stretching around them was shattering. Gabriel could hardly look at her. His optimism as he had set off earlier for her house now seemed pathetic and absurd. Even after he had been kicked in the face by her parents, he had still stupidly convinced himself that she would still be his. His wife. He had made the classic mistake of avoiding reality, which was that she was rich and he was poor and never the twain could meet. Whatever flimsy objections she was now trying to come up with.

'Don't say that,' Laura whispered. 'I love you.'

'Just not enough to prove it. Just not enough to marry me. Words without action are meaningless.'

'You make it sound so simple, Gabriel. You love me, therefore do as I say and follow me to the ends of the earth, never mind about hurting anyone along the way.'

He flushed darkly and his mouth tightened into a hard line. 'It is as simple as you choose to make it.'

'No, it's not! It's anything *but* simple! What about my university degree?'

'I told you...'

'Yes, that I could come to London and somehow it would all be sorted out! And my parents? Do I just walk away from them as well? Why can't you just...wait? Wait for a few years? My parents would adjust over time...I know they would. I would be able to finish my degree. Perhaps I could start in Edinburgh and arrange a transfer...' Her voice faltered into silence as she absorbed the hard expression on his face.

'I made a mistake.' His mouth curled into a twisted smile that was the death knell on any lingering illusions she might have been nurturing that she could somehow prevent him from walking out of that door and never turning back. 'I thought I knew you. I realise now that I never did.'

'You knew me, Gabriel. Better than anyone has ever known me,' Laura intoned dully. One errant tear slipped out of the corner of her eye and she let it trickle down the side of her face.

'Oh, I don't think so, *querida*.' The endearment that had filled her with joy only an hour before was now uttered with sneering cynicism. 'It's time for you to get back to the playground you know best. You will go to university and be the golden girl your mummy and daddy have trained you to be and then, in time, you will marry someone they approve of and live happily ever after.'

He turned away and began walking towards the door and that snapped her out of her daze and she rushed behind him, past him so that she could position herself in front, blocking his way out.

'Don't do this!'

'Get out of my way.' There was a grim determination in his voice but Laura stood her ground, refusing to watch him leave even though her head was screaming at her that it was all over and that there was nothing she could do to make him stay.

It flew through her head that she could agree to marry him. Marry him and crash headlong into her parents' disappointment and anger. Toss aside her aspirations and follow him, as he wanted, to the ends of the earth. But the moment was lost when she realised, knowing it to be a fact, that he would never accept her now. All those little indications of his pride that she had glimpsed over the months had solidified into something she could not breach.

She felt an anger rise inside her suddenly. 'If you loved me, you would wait for me.'

He reached out and pulled the door open from behind her and, tall though she was, she was not half as powerful as he was. He opened it easily, sending her skittering out of his path.

'It can't end like this,' Laura cried desperately. Her flash of self-righteous anger had lasted but a second before disappearing in a puff of smoke. 'Tell me that we'll meet again.'

He paused and looked at her then. 'You should hope, *querida*, that we never do...'

CHAPTER TWO

THIS was Gabriel Greppi's favourite time of the day. Six-thirty in the morning, sitting in the back seat of his Jaguar whilst his driver covered the forty-minute drive into London, allowing him the relative peace and sanity to peruse the newspapers at his leisure. From behind the tinted windows of the car, he could casually look out at the world without the world casually looking back at him.

Sometimes, in the quiet tranquillity of the car, he would occasionally reflect that the price he had paid for his swift and monumental rise to prominence had been a steep one. But such moments of reflection never lasted long. His days of idle, pointless introspection were long over and they belonged to a place he would never again revisit.

He picked up the *Financial Times* and began scouring it, his dark eyes frowning in concentration as he rapidly scanned the daily updates on companies and their fortunes. This was his life blood. Companies that had suffered under mismanagement, inefficiency or just plain bad luck were his playground and his talents for spotting the golden nugget amidst the dross were legendary.

He almost missed the tiny report slipped towards the back section. Four meagre square inches of newsprint that had him narrowing his eyes as he re-read every word written about the collapsing fortune of a certain riding stables nestling in the Warwickshire equestrian territory.

No, not a man for idle introspection, but this slither of introspection galloping towards him made his hard mouth curve into a smile. He reached forward and tapped on the glass pane separating him from Simon, his driver.

'You can take the scenic route today, Simon,' he said.

'Of course, sir.' Obligingly, Simon took the next turning from the motorway and began manoeuvring the byroads that led away from the country mansion in Sunningdale towards the city centre.

Whilst Gabriel relaxed back into the seat, crossed his long legs encased in their perfectly tailored and outrageously expensive handmade trousers, and clasped his hands behind his head.

So the riding stables were on the verge of bankruptcy, pleading for a buyer to rescue them from total and ignominious ruin. He could not have felt more satisfied if a genie had jumped in front of him and informed him that his every wish would come true.

For the first time in seven years he allowed his tightly reined mind to release the memories lurking like demons behind a door.

Laura. He stared through the window at the lush countryside gliding past them and lost himself in contemplation of the only woman to have brought him to his knees. The smell of the stables and the horses. Glorious beasts rising up in the misty twilight as they were led back into the stables. And her. Long white-blonde hair, her strong, supple body, the way she laughed, tossing her head back like one of her adored animals. The way she moved under his touch, moaning and melting, driving him crazy. The way she had finally rejected him.

His jaw clenched as he feverishly travelled down memory lane and he felt the familiar, sickening rush of rage that had always accompanied these particular memories.

'On second thoughts, Simon. Take the motorway. There's a call I want to make...'

Or rather, a call he would instruct his head accountant to make. But Andy, his head accountant, didn't get to the office until eight-thirty, and waiting until then nearly drove Gabriel to the edge of his patience.

It was not yet nine when Laura raced into the kitchen and grabbed the telephone, breathing quickly because she had just finished doing the horses and had opened the front door to the frantic trilling of the phone. Of course, the minute she picked up the receiver, she could have kicked herself. Why bother? She knew what was going to greet her from the other end. Someone else asking about unpaid bills. Lord, they were crawling out of the woodwork now! Her father had managed to keep the hounds at bay whilst he had been alive, spinning them stories, no doubt, and using his upper-crust charm to squeeze more time in which to forestall the inevitable, but the minute he had died and she had realised the horrifying extent of the debt, every man Jack had been down her throat, demanding their money. The house had been mortgaged to the hilt, the banks were clamouring for blood and that was only the tip of the iceberg.

How she had managed to swan along in total ignorance of their plight was now beyond her comprehension. How could she not have managed to realise? The house slowly going to rack and ruin? The racehorses being sold one by one? The horses in their care gradually being removed by concerned owners? She had merrily gone her way, doing her little job in the town, coming back to the security of her home and her horses, protected as she had always been from the glaring truth of the situation. God!

Her voice, when she spoke, was wary. 'Hello? Yes?'

'This is Andrew Grant here. Am I speaking to Miss Jackson? The owner of the Jackson Equestrian Centre?'

Laura ran her slender fingers through her shoulder-length blonde hair and stifled a little groan of despair.

'Yes, you are, and if you're calling about an unpaid bill, then I'm afraid you'll have to put it in writing. My accountant will be dealing with…with all unpaid bills in due course.' Like hell he would be. There was simply no money to deal with anything.

'I have in front of me an article in the *Financial Times* about your company, Miss Jackson. It doesn't make pretty reading.'

'I…I admit that there are a few financial concerns at the moment, Mr Grant, but I assure you that—'

'I gather you're broke.'

The bluntness of the statement took the wind out of her and Laura shakily sat on the old wooden chair by the telephone table. With the phone in one hand, she stared down at her scuffed brown boots and the frayed hem of her jeans. In the past four months she felt as if she had gone from being a carefree twenty-six-year-old girl to an old woman of eighty.

'Money is a problem at the moment, yes, Mr Grant, but I assure you—'

'That you will miraculously be able to lay your hands on enough of it to clear your debts, Miss Jackson? When, Miss Jackson? Tomorrow? The day after? Next month? Next year?'

'My accountant is—'

'I have already had a word with your accountant. He's managing your company's death rites, from what I gather.'

Laura gave a sharp intake of breath and felt her body tremble. 'Look, who *are* you? You have no right to make phone calls to my accountant behind my back! How did you get hold of his number? I could take you to court for that!'

'I think not. And I have every right to contact your accountant. The demise of your company is now public knowledge.'

'What do you want?'

'I am proposing a rescue package, Miss Jackson…'

'What do you mean by a "rescue package"? Look, I really don't know a great deal about finances. Perhaps it would be better if you contact Phillip again and then he can explain to me…'

'On behalf of a very wealthy client, who wants to meet with you personally to discuss what he has in mind.'

'M-meet with *me*?' Laura stammered in confusion. 'Phillip has all the books. It would be extremely unorthodox to—'

'The sooner you are able to arrange a meeting with my…ah…client, the quicker your problems will be resolved, Miss Jackson, so could I propose…' he paused and down the end of the line she could hear the soft rustle of paper '…tomorrow? Lunchtime?'

'Tomorrow? Lunchtime? Look, is this some kind of joke? Who exactly *is* this so-called client of yours?'

'You will have to travel to London for the preliminary meeting, I'm afraid. My client is an exceptionally busy man. If the deal shows promise, then, naturally, he will want to see the stables for himself. Now, there's a small French restaurant called the Cache d'Or just off the Gloucester Road in Kensington. Could you be there by one?'

'I…'

'And if you have any doubt as to my client's financial worthiness or, for that matter, the reliability of this proposed deal, then I suggest you call Phillip Carr, your accountant, and he should be able to set your mind at rest.'

At rest was the last place her mind was one hour later,

after she had called Phillip and plied him with questions about the identity of the apparent knight in shining armour who wanted to buy one desperately ailing riding stables in the middle of nowhere.

'He can't be serious, Phillip. You've seen the place! Once glorious, now a destitute shambles. Not even a good reputation left to trade on! Just an empty, sad shell.' Laura felt the prickle of tears welling up when she said this. She could hardly bear to remember the place when it had been in its heyday, when her mother had still been alive and everything had been all right with the world. When everything had been all right in *her* world, a lifetime ago it seemed.

'He's certainly serious at this point in time, Laura, and, face it, what harm is there in checking it out?'

'Did you manage to find out who exactly this man is?'

'I have simply been told that his estimated wealth runs into several million, if not more, and I've been given a succinct list of his various companies.' Phillip sounded unnaturally sheepish and Laura clicked her tongue in frustration. She and Phillip went back a long way. He was now about the only person she could trust and the last thing she felt she needed was his reticence.

'Why the secrecy?'

'Because he is considerably powerful and he says that it's essential that no one knows of this possible deal.'

'I don't understand.'

Phillip sighed, and she could imagine him rubbing his eyes behind his wire-rimmed spectacles. 'Look, meet the man, Laura. He might just save the day and you have nothing to lose. The fact is, without some kind of outside help you'll lose everything. The lot. House, contents, your precious horses, any land you have left. It's far worse than I originally thought. You're standing on quicksand, Laura.'

Laura felt a shiver of fear trickle down her spine. Thank heavens her father had not lived to see this day. However much he had squandered everything, she refused to hate him for it. He had been caught up in one long vortex of grief after her mother had died, and what had followed, the gambling that had been exposed, the addiction to alcohol that he had always been able to hide beneath his impossibly cheerful veneer, all of it had been his own sad response to emotional turmoil.

She became aware that Phillip was talking to her and she just managed to catch the tail-end of his sentence.

'…and the worse is yet to come.'

'What do you mean? How could things get any worse?'

'You could be held liable for some of his debts. The banks could descend on you, Laura, claim your earnings. If this man seems genuine, then be more than open-minded about his offer. Entice him into it. It could be your last chance. I frankly don't see anyone else taking it on.'

Twenty-four hours later, with those words ringing in her ears, Laura dressed carefully and apprehensively for what could turn out to be the biggest meeting of her life. Her wardrobe sparsely consisted of a mixture of working clothes, which she wore to the office where she held down an undemanding but reassuring job three days a week as secretary for an estate agency, and casual clothes, which took the brunt of her work with the horses and showed it. Sensible dark skirts, a few nondescript blouses and then jeans and baggy jumpers. She chose a slim-fitting dark grey skirt, a ribbed grey elbow-length cardigan with tiny pearl buttons down the front and her high black shoes, which escalated her already generously tall height to almost six feet.

Hopefully, this powerful businessman would not be too

short. Towering over a diminutive man would do her, she conceded wryly, no favours at all.

Her nerves were in shreds by the time she arrived at the restaurant, after two hours of monotonous travel during which she'd contemplated the gloomy future lurking ahead of her.

As she anxiously scanned the diners, looking for an appropriately overweight, middle-aged man reeking of wealth, Gabriel, removed to the furthest corner of the room and partially out of her sight behind an arrangement of lush potted plants resting on a marble ledge, watched her.

He had not known what to expect. He had awakened this morning positively bristling with anticipation. Not a sensation he had experienced in quite a while and he had relished it. Money and power, he had long acknowledged, didn't so much corrupt as they hardened. Having the world at your beck and call produced its own brand of jaded cynicism.

He sat back in his chair, watching her through the thick, rubbery leaves of the plants alongside him, and a slow smile curved his handsome mouth. Seven years and this moment was well worth waiting for. Yes, she had changed. No longer did she have that waist-length hair, which, released, had always been able to turn her from innocent young thing into something altogether more sexy. No, but the blunt, straight, shoulder-length hair suited her. His eyes darkened as they studied the rest of her. The lithe body, the full breasts pushing out the little, prim grey cardigan, the long legs. He felt a surge of violent emotion and deliberately turned away, waiting for her now, with his whisky in one hand.

He sat back in the chair and swallowed a mouthful of his drink, mentally following her progress as she was ushered towards his table.

Their eyes met. Brown eyes widening in disbelief clashing with coal-black, thickly fringed ones. Gabriel smiled coldly as she stood in front of him, casting one desperate glance back over her shoulder and then back to him.

'Gabriel? My God, how are you?' The residue of shock was still rippling through her body as Laura looked at the spectacularly handsome man lounging in the chair in front of her. She clutched the back of the chair and managed a small, tentative smile.

'So, Laura, we meet again.' His hard black eyes raked over her body with casual insolence before returning to her face, and continued to watch her over the rim of his glass as he took another sip of his drink. 'You seem a little…disconcerted.'

In fact, she looked as if she might faint at any moment.

'I wasn't expecting…I thought…' Laura stared back at him, transfixed by his face and those mesmerising black eyes that had always made her feel hot and unsteady. Had it been *seven years* ago? It seemed like just yesterday. She cleared her throat. 'When this meeting was arranged, I had no idea…'

'That you would be coming face to face with me? No, you wouldn't have.' Gabriel gave an indolent shrug of his broad shoulders. 'But I am being very rude. Sit down.' He watched as she hesitated fractionally, knowing what was going through her head. She didn't want to be here. If she could have, she would have fled the restaurant as fast as she could. But she couldn't. She was trapped by her own financial circumstances in a cruel twist of fate that not even he, in his most vengeful moments, could have conceived.

'Sit,' he ordered silkily, when she continued to hover by her chair like a frightened rabbit caught in the headlights of a fast-moving car. 'After all, as old *friends* we have much to talk about.' She still had that peculiarly en-

ticing air of innocence and sensuality. Her extreme blonde-
ness in combination with those large, almond-shaped chocolate-brown eyes had always been eye-catching because
they contrasted so sharply with the contained intelligence
on her face. For the first time, Gabriel lowered his eyes as
his body treacherously began to respond to her.

'What do you want, Gabriel?' A pink tongue flicked out
to moisten her dry lips, but she obeyed his order and cautiously slid into the chair.

'Why, I thought my accountant made it perfectly clear
what I wanted...' Gabriel beckoned a waiter across and
ordered a glass of white wine for her, Sancerre, then he
smiled lazily. 'After seven years I am finally able to offer
you a drink. A drink in a smart, fashionable and excruci-
atingly expensive restaurant. As many drinks as you would
like, as a matter of fact. Is that not extraordinary...?'

'I would have preferred mineral water.'

Gabriel ignored her small protest.

Did he know what he was doing to her? Yes, of course
he did, Laura thought shakily. It was pay-back time. She
felt a shiver of apprehension feather down her spine as she
was swamped by memories. God, he had been beautiful.
She slid her eyes surreptitiously to him. He still was.
Suffocatingly and excitingly masculine. All male. Every
pore of him breathed virile sexuality and he hadn't
changed. No, he *had* changed. Power and wealth had hardened the ferociously handsome features of his face and the
eyes staring at her were cold and assessing. A wave of
nausea rushed over her.

'You look a little pale. Take a sip of your wine.' His
voice snapped her out of her memories and brought her
crashing back to reality. 'Please accept my sympathies on
the death of your father,' he said, observing her coolly,
whilst his fingers stroked the side of his glass.

'Thank you.' Laura paused to take a sip of wine. 'I see you…you've done very well. I had no idea…'

'That a poor boy like me working to make ends meet so that he could afford to complete his university course would turn out good in the end?'

'That's not what I was going to say. How is your father?'

'Back in Argentina and doing very well.'

'And you? How are you? Are you married? Children?' In her head, he had never married. Laura realised, with shock, that he had been in her head ever since he had stormed out of her life. She had allowed herself to be persuaded by her parents that his disappearance had been for the best, that she had her future, that they had never been suited, that she would forget him in time, but she hadn't forgotten him. And her memories of him were still of the raw youth who had swept her off her feet. Not of this man sitting in front of her with the world at his fingertips.

Gabriel's jaw hardened. Married? Children? Those were dreams he had nurtured a long time ago, dreams he had uselessly expended on the woman floundering in the chair opposite him. He had been naïve enough at the time to imagine that she had shared those dreams. Until reality had kicked him in the face and he had been forced to swallow the bitter truth that he had been nothing but an amusing plaything for a rich young girl. Her dreams of happy families had not included wedding a poor Argentinian. Not enough class. His hand tightened around his glass and he quickly swallowed the remainder of his drink.

'No,' he said abruptly. He signalled to the waiter for menus and, after they had placed their orders, he sat back in his chair and loosely linked his fingers on his lap. 'So…our fortunes have changed, have they not? Seven years ago, eating out at a restaurant like this would have been out of my reach.' His dark eyes gave a quick glance around their expensive surroundings before returning to her face. 'Who would have ever imagined that here I would one day sit, with you opposite me, in the role of...what shall we call it, Laura? Penitent?'

'Why are you so bitter?' Laura's eyes met his and skittered away in a rush of helpless confusion. 'It's been years...' She sighed. 'Look, I don't want to rake over old ground. Phillip tells me that you're interested in buying the riding stables. I might as well warn you that they're not what they used to be.' She wished desperately that he would stop staring at her.

'Why am I so bitter...?' he mused. His voice was lazy and thoughtful, but his dark eyes were coldly hostile and a shiver of dread slithered down Laura's spine. 'Why do you *think* I'm bitter?'

'Because your pride was dented when...' Her voice faltered and she nervously tucked a loose strand of hair behind her ear.

'Say it, Laura,' he commanded silkily. 'After all, it has been a long time since we last set eyes on one another. What could be more natural than to go over old ground?'

'What's the point of all of this?' She whipped her napkin from her lap and flattened it with the palm of her hand on the table. 'Do you have any intention of buying the stables, Gabriel, or did you decide to get me here so that you could watch me squirm? Humiliate me because I once turned down your proposal of marriage?' There. It was out and they stared at one another in lengthening silence.

She would not allow him the satisfaction of playing cat and mouse with her. He had no intention of buying any stables. He had simply used that as a pretext to get her here so that he could spend a few hours watching her squirm because she had wounded his volatile, Argentinian pride.

'I'm going.' She stood up and scooped up her handbag from the table. 'I don't have to stay and suffer this.'

'You're not going anywhere!' His voice cracked against her like a whip and she glared down at the impossibly handsome, ruthless face staring back at her with narrowed eyes.

'You can't tell me what I can and cannot do, Gabriel!' She leaned over, squaring her hands on the table, her body thrust towards him. It was a mistake. It brought her too close to him, too close to that sexy mouth of his and, as if sensing it, he smiled slowly.

'Times really have changed, in that case,' he murmured, his black eyes flicking to her parted lips, then dipping to view the heavy breasts gently bouncing beneath the cardigan. 'I remember when I could tell you *exactly* what to do, and you enjoyed every little instruction, if I recall...'

Bright pink feathered into Laura's cheeks as their eyes tangled and she drew her breath in sharply.

'But...' he was still smiling, although his expression was cool and closed '...that's not what this is all about, is it? This is about the riding stables, which is why you are going to sit back down, like a good little girl. This is about your future, and believe me when I tell you that you have no choice but to endure my company.'

Laura felt all the energy drain out of her. He had the upper hand. Whatever card she pulled out of the pack, he carried the trump. The fact that he loathed the sight of her was something she would have to grit her teeth and put up with because he was right, she had no choice.

'That's better,' he drawled, when she had returned to her seat. 'Now, I propose that we discuss this over lunch in the manner of two civilised adults.'

'I am more than happy to do so, Gabriel. *You're* the one who's intent on dragging the past up at every opportunity.' She was still trembling as she sat back and allowed the large oval plate of filleted sole to be placed in front of her. It smelled delicious, but her appetite seemed to have utterly deserted her. 'Perhaps we could agree to call a truce on discussing the past,' Laura intoned tightly.

'You are not in a position to offer agreements on anything.' He had ordered the halibut and he dug his fork into the white flesh, savouring the delicate flavour. He should have been delighted to have won this round, to have pulled the plug on her outburst and forced her to obey him, but, aggravatingly, there was no such sense of satisfaction. He stabbed another mouthful of food into his mouth. 'But let us get to the matter in hand. What is the position with the riding stables?'

'You know what the position is. It's a mess. Phillip must have explained all of that to your accountant or whoever the man was who made the phone call.'

'How much of a mess?'

'A lot of a mess,' Laura confessed grudgingly and half-heartedly continued eating. Her stomach felt inclined to rebel at the food being shovelled into it, but she would not let him get to her again. 'The racehorses have all gone. Sold. Four years ago. Most of the other horses were removed over time. I still have a few, but I doubt I shall be able to hang onto them for much longer. And the house…well…it's still standing, but just.'

'What happened?'

'Are you really interested?' Her eyes flashed at him. She couldn't help it. 'Or do you want all the grisly details for your scrapbook on how much the Jackson family fell? So that you can chuckle over it in the years to come?'

'Now who is guilty of dragging the past up?' Gabriel

taunted silkily. 'I am not asking questions any interested buyer would not ask.'

'And are you *really* interested in buying, Gabriel?'

Good question. He had toyed with the idea. Andy had been appalled at the thought of investing money in a decrepit stables that would probably never show any return for the money ploughed in, arguing that such enterprises failed or succeeded by word of mouth and that, because Gabriel was not a part of the racing scene, it was doomed to failure. And Gabriel had been able to see his logic. He had also been unable to resist the opportunity to avenge himself for a rejection which he had carried inside him like a sickness for too long. But had he really been serious about buying the place?

Now, he realised that he was deadly serious. A couple of hours in this woman's company was not enough to sate his appetite. He looked at her, at the strong, vulnerable lines of her face and the supple strength of her body, and suddenly wondered what other men had touched her. He would touch that body again, he would feel it move under his hands, but this time unaccompanied by the emotions of a boy. He would touch her as the man he now was. He would take her and she would come to him on his terms and when he was finished with her, then *he* would be the one to reject her. If it took the purchase of the riding stables, then so be it. It was hardly as though he could not easily afford it.

'I am interested in buying,' he agreed smoothly. 'So explain what happened.'

'Mum died. That's what happened.' Laura closed her knife and fork and wiped her mouth. 'Her heart. We both knew that it was…that she was weak, but I think Dad just never accepted the reality of it. He always thought that something would come along, some magical potion and everything would be all right. But nothing came along, and when she died he just couldn't cope. He lost interest in the place. He said it all reminded him of Mum and he began going out of the house a lot. I thought it was to see horses, visit old friends. Since he died, I discovered it was to bet.' She sighed and pressed her fingers against her eyes, then propped her face in her hands and stared past Gabriel with a resigned, thoughtful expression. 'He gambled away everything. Amazing to think how quickly a thriving concern can go down the pan, but, of course, the world of horses doesn't operate along the same lines as a normal company. The racehorses were sold.'

'He gambled away *all* of the profits from those thoroughbreds?'

'Not all.' Laura's eyes slid towards him and she shivered. Despite the stamp of ruthlessness on his face, he still possessed bucket-loads of that sexual magnetism that had held her in his power. He was her enemy now and making no bones about it and she would rather have died than have let him see that he could still have an effect on her. 'He made two investments that were disastrous and plunged him even further into debt. I guess, that was when the spiral of gambling to win really began.'

'And you were not aware that all of this was going on?'

'I never imagined there was any reason to be suspicious!' Laura returned defiantly. 'I wasn't at home doing the books. How was I supposed to know that the money was disappearing?'

'Because you have eyes and a brain?'

That stung because it was the refrain that played over and over in her own head. But did he have to say it? But then, why shouldn't he? His past and present had now merged to give him the freedom to say whatever damn thing he wanted to and she could do nothing but accept it because she needed him. Her hand curled into a ball on her lap.

'Obviously not enough of either,' Laura said icily.

'What happened to your plans for becoming a vet?' Gabriel asked, abruptly changing the subject.

'I had to…to cut short university because of Mum and then…well…' She shrugged and lowered her eyes, not wanting to think about what might have been. 'Dad needed me.'

'You have been at home all these years? Helping out?' He sounded amazed and Laura flushed, remembering all her grand plans.

'Of course I haven't just been at home!' she snapped. 'I…I have a job in town.'

'Doing what?'

'Is this part of the normal line of questioning by any prospective buyer?'

'Call it curiosity.'

'I'm not here to satisfy your curiosity, Gabriel. I'm here to talk about the riding stables. There's still a bit of land and of course the house, but that's about it. It's all heavily mortgaged. Now, do you still want to proceed or not?'

'You're here to satisfy whatever I want you to satisfy and make no mistake about that. I know everything there is to know about the financial state of your riding stables and, without my money, life will be very bleak indeed for you. So if I ask you a question, you answer it. Now what job do you do?'

'I work in an estate agency, if you must know. I'm a secretary there. Since Dad died I've had to cut short my working hours so that I could spend more time at the stables, but I still work three days a week.'

And what a sight for sore eyes she must make in the place, Gabriel mused suddenly. Stalking around like one of those thoroughbreds she had spent her life looking after. Driving those poor, hapless men crazy.

'A secretary,' he said sardonically. 'What a disappointing end to all your ambitions.' His voice was laced with irony and Laura bit down the response to fly at his throat.

'I happen to like it there,' she said tautly.

'Satisfying, is it? As satisfying as it would have been to work with animals? Shifting bits of paper around a desk and fetching cups of coffee?'

'Some things are not destined. That's just the way life goes and I've accepted it.' Laura met his gaze stubbornly. She would never have guessed that her stormy, passionate lover could have transformed into this cold stranger in front of her. 'I may not have risen to dizzy heights and made lots of money like you, but money isn't everything,' she threw at him, and in response he gave a short bark of dismissive laughter before sobering up.

'At least not now,' he amended coldly. 'Not now that you have no choice but to fall back on that little homily, but somehow it doesn't quite sit right on your shoulders, Laura. Perhaps my memory is a little too long.' He leaned forward, planting his elbows on the table and closing the space between them until he was disconcertingly close to her. 'I remember another woman, to whom money was very important and maybe I have more in common with that woman now, because money *is* important, isn't it, *querida*? Money drove us apart and now it brings us together once again. The mysteries of life. But this time, I hold you in the palm of my hand.' He opened one hand before squeezing it tightly shut whilst Laura looked on in mesmerised fascination. 'Tell me, how does it feel for the shoe to be on the other foot?'

CHAPTER THREE

PHILLIP should have been handling this. Phillip should have been the one showing Gabriel around the stables and the house, gabbling optimistically about how much of a turnaround could be achieved with the right injection of cash. Wasn't that supposed to be a part of his job?

But Phillip was not going to be around. Away on business, he had apologised profusely. He had no idea why she was so intimidated at the thought of showing her prospective buyer the premises. It wasn't as if he were a complete stranger. And, after all, she *did* work in an estate agency, even if showing people around properties did not actually constitute one of her duties. She would be absolutely fine, he had murmured soothingly.

But Laura didn't feel fine. She had had precisely three days after that nerve-shredding meeting with Gabriel to realise that the last thing she felt about selling to him was fine.

The fact was she had not been able to get him out of her mind. In under half an hour, he would be driving up that long avenue towards the house, and she still didn't feel prepared. Either physically or mentally.

She had carefully collated all the paperwork given to her by Phillip in connection with the accounts for the riding stables and laid them out neatly on the kitchen table. She had tidied the house in an attempt to make it appear less shabby, although the sharp spring sunlight filtering through the long windows threw the faded furnishings into unflattering focus. She had taken her time dressing, forsaking the security of working clothes for the comfort of trousers and a loose checked shirt. She had still found herself with one and a half hours to spare.

Now, she waited with a cup of coffee, her stomach churning with tension and then twisting into knots when she finally spotted a sleek black Jaguar cruising slowly towards the house.

Laura took a deep breath and reluctantly responded to the ring of the doorbell, pulling open the door once her face had been arranged into an expression of suitably detached politeness. She had spent so many hours reminding herself that, as far as Gabriel Greppi was concerned, she was an object of dislike that she had automatically assumed that her body would obediently follow the dictates of her head and not react when she saw him. She was wrong. Her eyes flickered over him as he stood in front of her, casually dressed in a pair of khaki trousers and a short-sleeved shirt that revealed the dark, muscular definition of his arms. A faint perspiration broke out over her body and she stood back, allowing him to brush past her and then stand in the hall so that he could slowly inspect it.

'Did you...find the house okay?' Laura asked nervously, closing the front door.

'Why shouldn't I have?' The black eyes finished their leisurely tour of the hall and he looked at her with a cool expression.

'No reason. I collected most of the paperwork from Phillip. It's all in the kitchen, if you want to go and have a read.'

'In due course,' Gabriel drawled lazily. 'Right now, I'd appreciate something to drink and then you can show me around.'

'Of course.' She walked ahead of him and he followed her into the kitchen, appreciating the view of her long legs and well-toned body. He had had three days to savour his plans for seduction. Three days during which even the demands of his beloved work had paled into the background. The more he had contemplated it, the more beautifully just it had all seemed. One rejection deserved another and he had been given the opportunity to achieve it. The wheel had turned full circle and he would reap the benefits of sweet vengeance. Despite the massive control he applied in his working life, he was innately a man of passion, and his response to the situation did not disconcert him in the slightest. Laura was unfinished business and he would finish it at last, once and for all.

'What would you like to drink?' she was asking him, watching as he skirted around the large central island in the middle of the kitchen and towards the French doors that led out onto the open fields at the back.

'I assume there is some kind of structural report on the house amidst that stack of papers on the table,' he said, turning around to look at her.

'What kind of structural report?' Laura stammered, frowning.

'The kind that will tell me whether this house is in need of serious renovation, or whether its state of decay is confined to the superficial. You can appreciate that such information will necessarily reflect any price I might be willing to pay.'

'The house isn't falling down, Gabriel.'

'How do you know? These old properties need a lot of attention and, from the looks of it, it has had less than zero.'

'You're determined to rub it in my face, aren't you?' she asked tightly, moving over to the table so that she could begin sifting through the inches of paperwork to see whether she could locate anything about the material state of the house. She raised her eyes to his resentfully. 'You just can't resist reminding me that you could make or break me, can you?'

'Is that what I'm doing? I thought I was merely asking for information about the property.' He looked at the bruised, hurt eyes and felt a sharp twinge of something he did not want to feel. 'Leave it,' he said abruptly, 'it can wait. For now, I would very much like something to drink. Tea would be nice.'

'You never used to like tea.' The words were out of her mouth before she could think and colour slowly crawled into her face as she spun around and began fiddling with the kettle. God. Please. Don't let the past sneak up and grab me by the throat. 'How do you take it?'

'Very strong with one sugar.' Gabriel sat down at the table. That little stack of paperwork would just have to wait. He wouldn't be able to concentrate on any of it anyway. Not with her moving around in front of his roving eyes like that, reaching up to fetch mugs from the cupboard so that he could see a little pale slither of skin, as firm and as toned as if she were still the young girl of nineteen he had once completely possessed.

When she sat at the kitchen table, she made sure to take the chair furthest away from his, and gazed down at her fingers cradling the mug. The silence was excruciating. She could feel his eyes on her and she wondered what he was seeing. Certainly not the uninhibited young girl she had once been. Could he sense her fear? And if he did, would he know where it stemmed from? Would he guess that he terrified her because she was realising how much she still responded to him? Physically? As though the intervening years had never existed?

'When did your father…leave to return to Argentina?' she asked in a stilted voice, simply to break the silence.

A year after I completed my university course.' Gabriel stood up and Laura jumpily followed his movements with her eyes as he prowled through the kitchen, like a restless tiger moving as a way of expending its immense energy. 'He did not manage to find a satisfactory post to fill the one he had lost and he returned to be with the rest of his family. I went on to work at a trading house and discovered that I possessed a talent for working the stock market. A quite considerable talent. I was rewarded with the financial backup to start my own business.' He sipped some of his tea and directed a cutting smile at her. 'While your fortunes were falling, mine were on the rise. Is life not full of little ironies? But, I forgot, you would rather I did not mention my successes, which you can only view as a measure of your own failures. Or rather, those of your family.'

'That's not true. I'm very pleased for you.'

'Pleased because I am now in the position to rescue you from your financial mess?'

'Stop it, Gabriel!' She stood up and moved towards him, bristling with anger. 'You talk about discussing things like two civilised adults but that's the last thing you're interested in doing, isn't it? You haven't even glanced at all those papers on the table!'

'I told you. I'll look at them in due course. Not that it makes an appreciable difference. I know the state of your finances, Laura. You owe everyone money. I am stunned that the place continued to exist for as long as it has. But then, your father must have benefited from the fact that he was on personal terms with his bank manager, not to mention all his suppliers.' He sipped his tea and looked at her flushed face over the rim of his mug. 'What would you do if I decided not to buy?' he asked.

'I expect Phillip would find another buyer.'

'Really? Has he had much interest so far?'

'I don't know.' Laura stared down at him with her arms protectively folded across her chest.

He could see that she was braced for another attack and he resisted the urge to oblige. He would have her, but to have her he would have to gain her trust. She was right. He was not behaving like a civilised adult. Having prided himself over the years on his ability to remain aloof, to detach himself to a position from which he could dispassionately control his surroundings, he was now acting like an adolescent suffering from a severe bout of pique.

He drained the remainder of his tea and stood up. 'Shall we look around the rest of the house now?'

It was impossible not to be aware of him as they walked up the winding staircase that led to the first floor. Instead of following her, which would have been bad enough, he walked alongside her and the flanks of his muscular thighs were only inches away from brushing against hers.

Had he simply been a good-looking man, Laura was sure that she would have been immune to his predatorial charm. But she had once known and touched every inch of that powerful body, and the memory of it waged a silent and savage war inside her against the reality of the situation. He had come back into her life a hostile and aggressive stranger and she could not afford to allow nostalgia for the past destroy her sense of perspective.

Although the land around the house was extensive, Oakridge House itself was relatively small. Five bedrooms, all with individual fireplaces, two bathrooms and a nest of smaller rooms on the ground floor, the largest of which was the formal drawing room, which had not now been used for years.

Laura started with the guest rooms and she maintained a nervous silence as he slowly inspected each one in turn.

Then the bedroom that had once been shared by her parents.

'This house must have seemed very big when your mother died,' Gabriel commented, gazing around him at the floral curtains and matching bedspread, and the dressing table, which, though cleared of everything, still looked as though it were waiting for someone to sit at the stool and peer into the angled mirror. 'Did it not occur to your father that he should sell the place and retire on the generous profit he would have made? Instead of remaining here and squandering the lot?'

'I suggested it to him.' Laura remained by the door, rigid with tension. 'But he said that he couldn't bear to leave the memories behind.'

'Ah. So he did the next best thing by running the place into the ground.' He walked towards her, noticing the way she shrank away from him and it took a superhuman effort not to allow his surge of rage at that to cross his face. 'And how do you feel about living here now?' he quizzed as he walked towards her bedroom.

'I have no choice, as it happens.' Laura watched as he pushed open the door to her bedroom and stepped inside. This felt like the deepest invasion of her privacy, but even so she felt a betraying wave of emotion rush through her at the sight of him looking around him, looking at the bed she still slept on. 'I…no one is really interested in buying the house with all the stabling…' she found herself chattering on witlessly, just to stop her eyes from flicking towards the bed and imagining him lying there, naked, with her next to him. 'It…Phillip says that it's too isolated to appeal to families, who like…like being surrounded by other houses…the whole package seems to put them off…' Her voice trailed off as he walked towards her, impossibly sexy, his eyes fixed on her softly parted mouth.

Her eyes slid sideways, avoiding him, and she licked her lips nervously.

'So why not just cut up whatever land you have left and sell it to a building company? I am sure someone, somewhere, would love to erect thousands of little starter houses here.' He was now within touching distance of her and he could sense the tension oozing out of her. Was it sexual tension? he wondered. He leaned against the doorframe, so that he was now impossibly close to her.

'It's...it's green-belt land...and besides, Dad expressed the wish in his will that the place be sold lock, stock and barrel as riding stables.'

'How considerate of him, lumbering his only offspring with the burden of trying to find the buyer in a million. You seem a little edgy. Am I making you nervous?'

It would have given him a kick of satisfaction to know that he was the reason for her shallow breathing and fluttering eyelids, but, frustratingly, he realised that he was no longer the young man he once was, sure of her responses to him. For all he knew, she could be itching to escape his presence for completely different reasons. Trapped by the man she had once rejected and loathing the sight of him because he held her future in his hands. His lips thinned into a forbidding line.

'Of course not,' Laura breathed, inching away out into the corridor. 'But...but it's getting a bit late. Perhaps we ought to have a quick look around the stables...before the light fades...'

Gabriel pushed himself away from the door. Whatever she felt for him now, he would make sure that time worked its magic on her, time and his persuasive powers to seduce her back into his arms, back into his bed and towards the inevitable rejection. He would allow her to wriggle but then he would reel her in. He wondered how her body would feel after all these years, and felt himself harden at the thought.

'No need to show me the land,' he commented. 'Just the stables and, of course…the other outbuildings.' He saw her pause fractionally when he said this and he knew, with a fierce stab of undiluted satisfaction, that she was thinking the same thing that he was. The offices. Home of their stealthy love-making seven years ago. She might have eradicated him from her life when he had made a nuisance of himself by daring to propose marriage to her, but she still couldn't quite forget the passion they had shared, could she?

It was still light when they got outside, but he had not arrived till a little after four and the light was already beginning to fade.

'I only have the three horses left,' Laura was telling him, with her back to him as she walked past the empty stalls. 'Two are so old that they probably won't make it through this winter, and I really shouldn't be spending money on feeding them, but…'

'But you cannot bear the alternative.'

Laura turned to look at him, her eyes flashing with anger. 'That's right, Gabriel! I can't bear the thought of having them put to sleep! I know that it doesn't make financial sense and I suppose, to a man like you, anything that doesn't make financial sense isn't worth considering, but I'm afraid I've still got some compassion left!'

'Unlike me?' He looked at her and fought the urge to kiss her very firmly on that quivering pink mouth. God, even after all the muddy water under their bridge, he was still attracted to her! It confused him and confusion was not an emotion with which he had much familiarity.

'Unlike you!' she agreed with vehemence. 'You never used to be like this, Gabriel. What happened?' She had intended to throw that at him with scathing disdain, but instead she winced as she heard the genuine curiosity in her voice.

'Life happened,' he said abruptly.

'I'm surprised you never married.' A slight, cool breeze lifted her hair from her shoulders and Laura wrapped her slender arms around her body.

'Because I am such a catch?'

'You're good-looking and eligible. I would have thought that you would have had hundreds of women beating a path to your door in search of a band of gold.'

'Oh, but I have,' Gabriel drawled smoothly. 'I prefer my life to be uncluttered, however, so I usually try and end things before the beating-down of the door occurs.'

Of course he would have had numerous lovers, but she still felt a jolt of searing jealousy at the thought of them all, lying in bed with him, making love.

'Now, shall we continue with our tour of the empty stables? Or are there any more pressing questions you feel you need to ask?'

'I was simply being polite,' Laura muttered. 'If we're going to be doing business together, then we might as well be civil to one another, wouldn't you agree?'

'Doing business with one another?' He began strolling down the corridor that ran along the stabling blocks, peering into the forlorn, vacant stalls, seemingly checking each one for signs of imminent collapse.

'Hold on. We *are* doing business with one another, aren't we?' Laura hadn't budged and he eventually turned around to look at her. 'That's what all this is about, isn't it?' she persisted, her heart thudding as he slowly approached her. 'You *did* say that you were serious about buying the place, didn't you?'

'I also said that it would depend on its condition. I'm a

businessman first and foremost, as you were at such pains to point out. It's hardly likely that I'm going to throw my money into a pit from which I shall never be able to recover any of it, wouldn't you agree?' His mouth curved into a smile and Laura gave a little shrug of her shoulders, uneasily aware that he was toying with her even though what he had said was absolutely true and would have been said by any prospective buyer. Anyone would demand to see the goods and approve them if they were to invest money.

'My horses are just along here,' she said, leading the way. 'I know the stables look a bit desolate, but with sufficient money they can easily be brought up to standard.'

'Is that the selling blurb your accountant asked you to give me?'

'It's the truth.'

'They're a far cry from how they used to be seven years ago,' Gabriel remarked, pausing when she did to look at one of the older horses. He watched and saw the suspicious glitter in her eyes give way to tenderness as she pushed open the stable door and began stroking the horse. He could hear her murmuring under her breath.

'Did you keep Barnabus?' he asked softly, stepping into the darkened stable beside her and running his hands along the flanks of the horse whilst his eyes remained fixed on her down-turned head. He was assailed by a sudden rush of memories and breathed in sharply, tearing his eyes away from her just as she raised hers to his face.

'He's two stalls along.' She stood up and her expression resumed its wariness as she led him out, shutting the door behind her.

'It must be a bitter pill to swallow...all this...' The words were jerked out of him and her wary expression deepened.

'What do you think, Gabriel?' This time she didn't enter either of the stalls, standing well back when Gabriel walked in to run his long fingers over Barnabus's black head. It was too painful to watch.

'What do I think…?' he mused, leaving the stall with reluctance. Riding was in his blood. He would have liked to have mounted the stallion and ridden him across the fields, but there were more pressing things to do. 'I think…' he continued speculatively as he walked slowly towards the offices, making sure that he kept as close to her as he reasonably could—he wanted to make sure that she felt his presence '…that you find yourself in an impossible situation. This is your home, you have grown up here, the riding stables formed part of your childhood. I think you would do pretty much anything to hang onto them. Am I right?' They had reached the offices but, before entering, he turned to look at her.

'Naturally, I would like to see them brought back up to the standard they once were…' Laura responded hesitantly, not really knowing where this was going.

'Of course you would.' He smiled coolly at her. 'Because the alternative would be disastrous for you personally, wouldn't you agree? No roof over your head, for a start.' He pushed open the office door and stepped inside.

Just as he remembered. A little shabbier, but by far the least run-down of all the buildings. He paused in the middle of the room and looked at her over his shoulder. 'Come inside, Laura, and shut the door behind you. It's getting a little cold out there.' He turned his back to her and heard the soft click of the door being shut.

From the outer reception room, he strolled into the office, still there with its desk and files and the sofa, spread against one wall. He could sense her standing by the door, hovering, waiting for him to complete his perusal of the room, and he wondered savagely whether she had ever really missed him. She would have come into this office after he had left, and thought…what? Anything? Would she have felt some twinge of regret and wistfulness? Or would any such emotions have been quickly and easily replaced by relief that he had walked out of her life before he had become too much of a liability?

The thought of that made him clench his fists in his trouser pockets. He turned very slowly around until he was looking at her with a veiled expression.

'So tell me, Laura, what *would* you do to hang onto this place? And keep your lifestyle intact? I mean, three days a week working as a secretary surely cannot pay you very much. What would you be able to afford to buy in town? Or even to rent, for that matter? A one-room studio flat somewhere? Maybe you might be forced to share a house with someone…'

Laura eyed him uneasily as he casually strolled closer towards her. Every muscle in her body had tensed and she could hear herself breathing quickly, drawing in shallow bursts of air, which seemed barely sufficient to keep her standing on her wobbly feet.

Gabriel extended his arms, propping himself against the wall and trapping her so that she was forced to look at him, could barely move without colliding with some part of his aggressively masculine body.

'I…I haven't really…given it much thought…' she stammered as his black eyes bored into her.

'Well, think about it now.' He allowed her a few seconds of silence whilst he continued to stare at her. 'Having the bank repossess the place. You would get a pittance, you know. Probably enough to cover some of the debts but certainly nothing left over on which you could reasonably live. You might even be forced to pay off some of the creditors out of your own meagre personal funds. So…what would you do to hang on here?' His eyes dropped to her trembling mouth, then down to her breasts, which were heaving as she inhaled deeply to gather her self-composure, which had been blown to the four winds.

'Wh-what do you mean?' Her voice was little more than a choked whisper. Her glazed eyes couldn't leave his face.

'I mean that I still want you…' He removed one hand and shockingly placed it lightly at her waist, slipping it under her shirt so that he could run his finger along her waistline.

'I don't come with the property, Gabriel.' She could have accompanied that assertion with a forceful push, but for some reason Laura found that her hands were powerless to move.

'Ah, but would you *like* to?' His hand slipped further up the shirt until he could feel the weight of her breasts pressing heavily against his fingers. Her eyes were fighting him, but her body was singing a different tune, he realised. Her body still remembered what it felt like to be joined with his.

And his, he thought with a blow of startling clarity, had never forgotten. The women he had slept with during those intervening years had never fulfilled him the way this woman quivering under his touch had. The thought angered him and made his resolve harden. He cupped one breast in his hand and gently massaged it. Her breasts, like ripe, succulent fruit, had always turned him on and they were turning him on now. God, he could feel his erection stiffening in response.

'You can't buy me, Gabriel.' Laura's voice did not convey a convincing message of denial. Her nipples hardened into taut peaks of arousal, betraying her every instinct to run away as fast as she could from this man.

'Are you telling me that I don't turn you on, Laura? If that is what you're saying, then I don't believe you.' To prove his point, he rubbed the pad of his thumb over her throbbing nipple and smiled like a cat suddenly in possession of a large saucer of cream. Yes, she felt the same. His hands, which had caressed other bodies, now felt as though they had been designed to mould just this one. He dipped into the lacy covering and scooped out one large breast and felt a fierce kick of pleasure as a small moan escaped her lips. Lips that were begging to be kissed. Just as her nipples were begging to feel the pressure of his fingers playing with them, rubbing them until they ached with sensitivity.

He lowered his head and his mouth met hers with a hunger that he hadn't realised he had. His body pushed hers back against the wall and with a groan of sheer yearning Laura twined her arms around his neck, her tongue feverishly and urgently clashing with his.

Oh, yes, it felt good to taste him again. She was still reaching for him when he pulled away and she slowly opened her dazed eyes.

'Still the same fiery woman,' he murmured, drawing away and leaving her to hurriedly try and resurrect some of her scattered wits. Laura looked at him with her arms folded protectively across her breasts. Her heart was still thudding wildly behind her ribcage, but reality was beginning to sweep away the cloud that had made her fling caution to the winds.

He had kissed her to prove a point and prove it he had in no uncertain terms.

Gabriel could see the conflicting emotions race across her face like shadows but he felt no real sense of satisfaction. So she still wanted him, had not been able to resist him the minute he had laid his hand on her, but he wanted more. More than just the knee-jerk reaction afforded by two people obviously still attracted to one another. He wanted her body and soul.

'If you think I'm going to come to bed with you so that you buy this place, then you're mistaken, Gabriel.' Her words snapped him out of his reverie during which he had been thinking of her standing before him, naked, willing and ready to do whatever he wanted. Until the time came when he turned her away.

'I would not dream of asking any such thing of you,' Gabriel replied, lowering his eyes. 'You will come to bed with me because you still want me.'

'I hate you, Gabriel,' Laura whispered and in that moment she did. Hated him for being able to control her after all this time. He had once spoken about marriage and setting up house together, but on his terms. Even then, she doubted that he had known the meaning of love, love as something beautiful to be shared and for which sacrifices had to be made. He had wanted her enough to make her his possession, but had not loved her sufficiently to wait, to allow her to ride the storm of her parents' disapproval in her own time, to gain the qualifications that would have meant everything to her.

It had all become apparent over time that wanting someone was not enough. And now here he was, wanting her again but allied to that urge to possess, to take what he wanted, was a cruel streak that desired retribution for the damage she had done to his pride.

Yes, she hated him, she told herself fiercely, or, at least, she desperately needed to hate him.

Her utterance was like a knife twisting in his stomach. 'I do not know why,' he said acidly, 'when I am prepared to rescue you from your situation.'

'If you buy this place, then you're doing it for yourself,

Gabriel. What will you do with it? Convert it into a leisure centre? Turn it into a country house so that you have somewhere to spend weekends away from London? Or do you really care what happens to it? Will it just be enough to know that for a moment in time you could indulge your desire to have control over me?' She pulled open the office door, desperate to get out of the place and away from his suffocating masculine presence.

'I already own a country house,' Gabriel drawled, watching her retreat and allowing her the temporary victory of imagining that her retreat might be permanent.

'You don't live in London?'

'Naturally, I have a penthouse there for when I have to stay in the city, but my primary residence is in the country.'

Laura edged out of the room and into the cooling air outside. He followed her and she angled around him to lock the office door, pulling back so that she could create some vital distance between them as they walked back to the house.

'And you…you commute to London every day?' Keep the conversation on an impersonal level, she told herself feverishly. 'It…it must be exhausting.'

'I live in Berkshire. It's not a million miles away from London and, at any rate, I have a driver who takes me in to the city. Except, of course, when I decide to stay in my apartment in Chelsea.'

'If you're working late?' The house was thankfully within sight and Laura had never been more grateful to see it.

'Working late or…playing late,' he murmured, sliding his eyes across to her and watching as two bright patches of colour appeared on her cheeks.

Playing late. There was no need for him to expand on

that. Laura could well visualise the type of games he played and the sort of women he played them with. Sophisticated, beautiful women, the female counterparts of himself.

'So what would you do with the place?' she reverted to her original question.

'Allow me.' His hand brushed hers as he pushed open the front door and Laura felt an alarming quiver of sexual awareness race through her veins, making her jerk back. He stood aside and she scuttled past him into the hall.

'I would keep it as a riding stables, of course,' he harked back to her original question. 'It would require a considerable amount of money to bring the place back up to a respectable standard, but it is feasible.'

'And when do you think you'll be able to give me an answer on, uh, whether you're interested in buying or not?'

'After I've looked at all the paperwork,' Gabriel said lazily. 'Which reminds me, I need to get it all from the kitchen.'

'Uh, yes, of course. I'll just go and fetch it.' Anything to get away from him so that she could clear her head! She hastily gathered all the paperwork together and was rushing, head down, back into the hall, intent on shoving the lot into his hands and escorting him to the front door post-haste, when she more or less catapulted into him coming towards her.

The shock made her stumble and he caught her, wrapping his solid arms around her body to steady her.

'What are you doing?' she shrieked, pulling back and instantly regretting her desperate outburst as his coal-black eyes raked over her flushed face. She could have sworn that the devil could read every panic-driven thought in her head!

'You came hurtling out of that kitchen like a bullet,' he

said drily, propelling her gently back but keeping his hands firmly on her arms. Her face was flushed with defensive anger, which was slowly replaced by the dawning realisation that she had overreacted to his simple attempt to prevent them both from crashing to the ground. Like it or not, he thought with grim satisfaction, he was turning her world on its head. She might feel nothing for him emotionally, but he had awakened a dormant passion and if she thought that he was going to allow it to go away without first getting exactly what he wanted, then she was in for a shock.

'The papers?' She was looking at him in a dazed fashion. Now she blinked as he reminded her of the reason she had been rushing out of the kitchen and she quickly thrust the lot into his hands. 'I'll be in touch…soon.'

CHAPTER FOUR

LAURA sat at her desk, staring ahead at her computer screen and trying to focus on what was in front of her. Some agreement about a house that had just been sold. She had just typed it, but she really didn't have much of a clue as to what she had actually typed.

Three days and still no phone call. Phillip had told her that he would make the call to Gabriel on her behalf, to find out what his intentions were for buying the stables, and she had hotly denied him permission to do any such thing. She would not beg. She would not encourage Gabriel's notion that she was so desperate for him to purchase that she would do anything. Her behaviour three days previously, when she had fallen into his arms like a sex-starved nymphomaniac, still terrified her because she could see it happening again. And she would have to fight against any such thing with every bone in her body.

Lord, she had spent so long trying to expunge him from her mind. When he had walked out of her life, she had been desperate with grief, but she had hidden her desperation well. Her mother's health had been failing, and her father had already told her in no uncertain terms that any shock might prove the final straw and running after Gabriel Greppi would surely constitute shock. She had listened to them, aching and silent, and their soothing words that it was all for the best, that she was young, that she had her whole life ahead of her, that their two worlds could never meet and he was from a different world from the one she knew, had gradually numbed her into staying put.

And at the back of her mind grew the nagging suspicion that if he had truly loved her, he would have understood why she had refused his proposal. She had pleaded with him to stay and he had abandoned her. Then her mother had died and everything had slowly gone into free fall.

Seeing him again had been more than a shock, and realising the depth of his hatred for her even greater. But far more shocking was the fact that when he had touched her, every fibre in her body had burned and come alive and she had responded. God!

She printed off the letter in front of her, determined not to let him invade her mind, and was scanning Hugo's spidery handwriting to begin another letter when the door clanged open and she looked up to see the object of her fevered thoughts standing in the doorway. It was so unexpected a vision that she had to blink several times, convinced that the darkly sexy shape framing the doorway was an illusion.

No chance. Not unless everyone else in the office was simultaneously having the same illusion because a quick glance around showed six faces all turned in his direction and Hugo was briskly exiting his office, hands outstretched, obviously sensing someone with a lot of purchasing power.

Gabriel's black eyes found hers but he remained where he was, his sheer presence rendering total silence amongst her normally garrulous colleagues.

'Do come in! I'm Hugo, Hugo Ross. Come in, come in!' Hugo's booming voice broke the silence and they all returned to what they were doing. All except Laura, who could feel a sizzle of treacherous excitement exploding in her veins as Gabriel continued to watch her bewildered face.

'Hugo.' His voice was drily polite, but he did manage

to tear his eyes away from her sufficiently to concentrate on the blandly handsome man bearing down towards him. 'I hate to disappoint you, but I'm not in the market for a house…'

To be fair, Hugo took the disappointment well. He fell back and shrugged with a rueful smile. Gabriel was well aware that she was stunned to see him here where she worked. He was no longer looking at her but he could sense her eyes on him, wondering, no doubt, what decision he had come to in connection with the stables.

'Are you quite sure? We have some glorious properties around just at the moment.' Laura had seen that Hugo had already sized up the cut of Gabriel's cloth and she had no doubt that those glorious properties would begin at the million pound mark.

'I'm sure you do,' Gabriel returned smoothly, 'but I'm here on personal business.'

All eyes swivelled interestedly onto her as she stood up and plastered a bland smile on her lips.

'Hugo,' she said, moving into action and searingly aware of Gabriel's dark eyes riveted on her. 'This is Gabriel Greppi. Remember I told you that he might be interested in buying the stables?'

'Ah, yes, so you did.' This time Hugo's blue eyes were speculative as they focused on Gabriel. He was well aware of the extent of the financial difficulties hanging over the stables and Laura could see him making a careful judgement of the man in front of him. Judgement of the man as her prospective rescuer and of the man as simply a man and she felt a twinge of sympathy for him.

He had employed her initially as a favour to her father and they had become friends and he had made it clear that they could be more than just friends if she'd wanted. She had not and he had taken her refusal in good spirit, proving in the end to be one of the steadiest friends she had had over the years.

'I thought you might have telephoned,' she addressed Gabriel, 'or perhaps called Phillip to let him know…'

'Oh, I prefer to deal face to face with you in this matter.' He turned to Hugo with an icily polite smile. 'If you don't mind, Laura and I will discuss this matter in private. Get your bag,' he told her and, when she glanced uncertainly towards Hugo, he repeated the command, leaving her no choice but to obey.

'What time will you be back, Laura?' Hugo pointedly turned his back to Gabriel, a gesture that did not appear to disconcert Gabriel in the slightest. Hugo placed his hand on her arm with a look of concern on his face and over his shoulder Laura met Gabriel's stony expression with bland disregard.

If he thought that he could purchase her with the property, then he was wrong, and he was doubly wrong if he thought that he could control who touched her and who didn't. He might be pulling her out of a quagmire not of her making, but that didn't make him her saviour. Just the opposite, she thought, and a cold shudder of apprehension trickled down her spine.

'She'll be back when she's back and only to collect her things,' Gabriel announced shortly, moving around so that he was standing beside them both.

'I beg your pardon?'

'You heard me, Laura. I am taking you out to lunch to discuss my decision and you will not be returning to this job here.'

'Don't be ridiculous!' The door clanged open and a couple walked inside, holding hands and looking bright-eyed and optimistic. First-time buyers. Hugo, torn between sorting out the dramatic situation unfolding before him and seeing to the young couple, who were shortly followed by an elderly man and his wife, reluctantly left them alone.

'I am not being ridiculous,' Gabriel informed her with no effort to lower his voice.

'Shh! Gabriel,' she hissed, 'I can't just walk out of here and never return.'

'You *will* return. I told you—to collect your things.'

'Will you keep the volume down?'

Gabriel felt his lips twitch as he took in her flustered face. 'You never did like scenes,' he mocked. 'And, no, I will not keep my voice down, so, in order to avoid one, I suggest you do as I say.'

And with Hugo now glaring at her whilst trying to placate his prospective buyers that the dark, handsome man with the arrogant tilt of his head did not actually work for him, Laura resigned herself to grabbing her bag from the chair and stalking out of the office, ahead of him.

'How dare you?' She turned on him the minute they were outside, hands on her hips and her body thrust forward in a stance of pure aggression.

'How dare I come up here with the glad tidings that I am going to buy your riding stables? I thought you would have been overjoyed to see me.' He had thought nothing of the sort. He had known precisely what her reaction would have been to look up and see him standing there in her cosy little workplace. But he had discovered that he'd wanted to see where she worked. Another piece of the jigsaw that was slowly coming together to form the complete picture.

'You know what I mean, Gabriel!'

'Where do you want to go for lunch? I will rely on you to suggest somewhere quiet where we can have a talk…about business.'

'I'm not hungry!'

'Well, I am. So humour me.' With that he began striding along the high street, attracting stares from most of the women who walked past him, bar those too old or too young to notice.

Laura half ran until she caught up with him. Tall she might be, but her strides were no match for his, especially in her slightly heeled court shoes, which she was not accustomed to wearing.

'What about this place?' He stopped in front of a spacious wine bar that advertised its specials of the day with a blackboard on the pavement.

'You can't make me give up my job, Gabriel!'

He ignored her and she wanted to literally scream with frustration. If this was his primitive, caveman way of getting his own back on her after seven years, by controlling every aspect of her life, then he was doing a very good job of it, she thought furiously.

'We'll talk inside,' he informed her, glancing back at her flushed face over his shoulder as he stood aside to allow her to walk past him into the wine bar.

Laura maintained a simmering silence as they were shown to a table towards the back of the wine bar and handed two oversized menus, which she barely glanced at.

'Is it all right for me to talk now?' she asked sarcastically, leaning forward so that her breasts rested against the surface of the table and her straight, impossibly fair hair swung around her face.

'Just so long as you don't raise your voice. We wouldn't want to create a scene.' He glanced across at a waitress, who almost tripped over her feet in her haste to get to their table and take their drink order. Champagne. To celebrate. To which Laura automatically replied that she never drank alcohol at lunchtime since it made her feel sleepy.

'Does that matter? You are more than welcome to fall

asleep in my car on the way to the house. Once you have collected your possessions from your office and said a rueful goodbye to your fellow employees.' Not to mention your employer, Gabriel thought to himself, recollecting the hand on her arm and the expression of fondness in Hugo's eyes when he had looked at her. The thought that there might be something going on there made his lips tighten and he forced himself to relax. He would get to that later.

'I am not going to be leaving my job, Gabriel. That was not part of the deal.'

'It is now.' He sat back to allow their waitress to place two champagne flutes on the table and waited until she popped open the bottle and poured them both some of the bubbly golden liquid. 'After I had a look around the stables, well, I was frankly alarmed at their state of disrepair. You may not have noticed, but there are cracks on the ceilings, what looks suspiciously like rising damp in some of the rooms, not to mention parts of the roof that look as though they have exceeded their sell-by date by several years.' He played with the stem of his champagne flute, allowing his words to hit home and settle in, then he took a leisurely sip of his drink and proceeded to run his finger lightly and absent-mindedly around the rim of the glass.

'Naturally, I will have to have the place professionally surveyed, but I estimate the house alone will cost thousands in terms of refurbishment, and that is not taking into account possible structural faults.' He leaned back into his chair and linked his fingers loosely on his lap. 'A massive job.' He shook his head. 'I very nearly decided against buying, but…' Actually, he had thought no such thing. The sweet challenge of winning her back only to discard her was too irresistible.

Laura gulped down a generous mouthful of champagne and almost choked in the process.

'I still don't see what all of this has to do with my job,' she persisted in a panicky voice. 'I am very grateful that you've decided to buy the stables and you can sort out all the ins and outs with Phillip, but…' She trailed off into helpless silence as he sat there, politely listening to her and shaking his head in the thoughtful manner of someone dealing with a person who was missing something glaringly obvious.

'You're part of the bargain, Laura.'

'What do you mean? I'm not part of any bargain. I have my own life…'

'Oh, but you don't.' There was a cutting smoothness to his tone that she didn't like. *What did he mean that she was part of the bargain? Did he think that he was going to sleep with her, have her as his concubine or else no deal?*

'I don't understand.'

'Well, then, I had better explain, hadn't I?' But he would take his time, watch her stewing over his words, watch her wondering whether he intended to make her into a sex slave as a fair exchange for digging her out of the hole in which she had become submerged. *Sex slave.* The thought filled him with sudden warmth and he leaned forward, instantly invading her space. 'The sort of business that your family was involved in does not operate along the same lines as a normal company, as you yourself pointed out. For a start, it can only work if the person in charge knows about horses and, more importantly, knows people within the world of horses and horse-racing. Are you beginning to get my drift here?'

Only too clearly. 'There are plenty of people around who would jump at the chance of working for you. I could easily put you in touch with them.'

'But my solution rests a lot closer to home than that…'

He smiled with dangerous intent. 'Who better to help reconstruct the tatters of the riding stables than yourself, Laura?' He beckoned the waitress across and, having treated her to a full-wattage smile of pure charm, gave his lunch order and waited in polite silence whilst Laura stammered out hers, frankly the first thing she could spot on the menu.

'Another glass of champagne?' He tipped some more bubbly into her empty glass and said soothingly, 'There's no need to look so worried. I have absolute confidence in you.'

'That's not what's worrying me, Gabriel...'

'Is it not? What, then?' He inclined his head to one side and frowned in supposed puzzlement. Laura could easily have tipped her glass of champagne over his arrogantly beautiful head. He knew precisely what she was worried about. She was worried about the trap that she felt slowly closing in around her, but she knew that to mention any such thing would have him throwing back his head and roaring with laughter. He would deny any such thing, would accuse her of being melodramatic, and to all intents and purposes he would have good reason because what he was offering her was a generous deal with the opportunity to remain living under her own roof and helping to resurrect the riding stables she had grown up loving.

On paper, it all sounded wonderful. In practice, a little voice was issuing warnings at a rate of knots.

'Perhaps I could help out in my spare time,' she conceded lightly. 'I'm sure Hugo would be flexible with my hours, if I needed to have time off now and again.'

'Not good enough, Laura. Getting the stables back up to running standard is going to be a full-time job and you know it. People are going to have to be employed, contacts are going to have to be revived...' And the thought of her popping out to do her job with Hugo there to mop up any flagging spirits would not do at all. In fact, the mere thought of it made his stomach clench in violent knots.

'I will ensure that you are paid handsomely for your work, of course…'

'So in other words, I shall become your employee.'

'If you want to put it like that.'

'Is there another way of putting it?'

'You could see it simply as being offered the chance of a lifetime to get the stables back on the map where they belong…'

'In other words, I have no choice.'

'Naturally you have a choice. We all have choices. You can choose to reject my offer, in which event I shall be forced to return to London empty-handed.'

So in other words, no choice. Laura sighed and gulped down a bit more of the champagne. She could already feel it going to her head but she didn't care.

'So what happens next?'

'You mean after you go and collect your things from work?'

'After I go and tell Hugo what's happening. I don't *have* anything at work, as such.'

'He already knows what is happening.' Gabriel narrowed his eyes on her flushed face. God, but how he would have liked to have plunged straight into her beautiful head and found out what exactly was going on in there. He couldn't imagine her being attracted to a man like Hugo, making wild love with him, but then maybe she now liked them safe and bland and unexciting.

'I don't intend to disappear without any sort of explanation to him. I've worked there for years now and he's been…good to me…'

'And in what ways has he been "good to you"?' Gabriel's mouth twisted and Laura glared back at him.

'You have a one-track mind.'

'I recall a time when you liked that...' he murmured, and she couldn't help it. A faint pinkness invaded her cheeks. Oh, yes, she remembered that time well. Too well.

'That was then and this is now,' Laura informed him crisply. 'After I quit my job, what then?'

'What then? Why, we sign papers. Mine are all prepared, including the stipulation that you work for me running the place. I can have them faxed to your accountant by lunchtime tomorrow. More immediately, we return to the house. My surveyor is booked to inspect it this afternoon. As soon as the deal is signed, I can begin throwing some food to the baying wolves and you can begin sleeping easier at night knowing that the bailiff will not be knocking at your front door.'

Their food arrived but all Laura could do was toy with the Caesar salad on her plate. Her mind was buzzing with thoughts, most of them vaguely alarming.

'You should eat more than that,' she heard him saying and Laura blinked in surprise at the sudden change in conversation. One minute informing her that he was now in charge of her life, or at least a hefty part of it, and the next minute chiding her for not eating enough for all the world as if they were two normal people, having a normal conversation in a normal situation.

'Is salad all you have been living on since your father died?'

'Why do you ask?' Laura retorted suspiciously, only to sigh at her overreaction to a perfectly polite question. 'It's easier.' In fact, she had lost weight since her father had died. Everything had fallen on her shoulders and somehow rounding up the day with a hearty meal for one had not been top of her agenda.

'You've lost weight.'

'Since when?'

'Since I last made love to you seven years ago.'

Laura nearly gagged on the bluntness of his statement. Had he done that on purpose? Because he knew that it would send her entire nervous system into a rapid nose-dive? But when she looked at him, it was to find him returning her gaze with complete innocence.

'I happen to like the way I look,' she retorted. 'You're entitled to your own taste in women if you like them plump.'

'Voluptuous,' Gabriel corrected mildly.

'I was never voluptuous, so your tastes must have changed over the years!'

'Oh, you were. Curves in all the right places…breasts a man could fill his hands with.' His voice was low and lazy and at the mention of her breasts he openly looked down at hers before flicking his dark eyes back to her flushed face. 'Your breasts at any rate are still as wonderfully bountiful as they used to be…'

'This is a ridiculous conversation,' Laura choked hotly. 'We were supposed to be discussing business.'

'We were. Now I thought we might move on to more general conversation.'

'If your idea of general conversation is discussing my figure, then…then…'

'Then…?'

'Then you're wasting your time because I'm not going to join in!'

'Perhaps it *was* a little rude of me, but really, you need to take care of yourself. I don't want you collapsing on me when you need to have all the strength at your disposal to deal with the work ahead.'

'Have you got some sort of...plan...or timetable?' Laura grasped the opportunity to steer the conversation away from the dangerously personal observations he had just thrown at her. She was mortified to discover that, unwittingly, he had stirred something inside her that had had her melting, thinking thoughts best kept hidden.

'You're the one in the know when it comes to horses. What do you suggest?' She was making a big effort to calm down. The blushing hue of her cheeks was subsiding and her normal colour was returning, but she still couldn't quite meet his eyes. Gabriel watched it all and he realised that at least part of his pleasure, if not all of it, was derived from the knowledge that he was getting under her skin. He also realised that he *wanted* badly to get under her skin, that his purely male response to her went beyond any desire for revenge. He wanted to taste the sweetness of that full mouth once again. That brief moment of passion three days earlier had only served to tease his appetite and to remind him of how intensely satisfying the act of making love had been with her.

He dragged his mind back to what she was saying and realised that he had been staring at her with an utterly blank expression when she tilted her head to one side and frowned.

'Are you listening to me?'

'Oh. Yes. Of course. You were saying...?'

Was he so bored that he couldn't even keep his mind focused on what she had just spent five minutes rattling on about? Laura wondered.

'I was saying that I can get in touch with all our old suppliers and hopefully convince them that they can resume doing business with us again. But before then, I would have to begin the process of wooing old clients back. Some of them will have gone for good, but I personally know a few who were truly sad about…about the way things turned out and privately told me that if ever the business picked back up, they would return their horses. God, Gabriel…it's such a huge job. I just don't know…'

Her eyes clouded over and he found that he didn't like that. He almost preferred the resentment to the sadness. Not, he reminded himself grimly, that the disintegration of the stables had anything to do with *him*, but he felt a sudden rage for the old fool who had done this to his daughter.

'You can do it,' he said gently. 'If anyone can do it, you can. I have utmost faith in you, Laura.'

'But I have no real idea where to start. There's so much…' She chewed her lip, fighting back the overwhelming urge to burst into tears. His anger she could handle. She didn't like it but, in a funny way, she understood it. His gentleness she found much more disconcerting, as she found her own sudden temptation to lean on him, get strength from him, let him hold her and soothe her problems away.

I must be mad, she thought shakily. He declared himself the enemy and made no bones about it. How on earth can I be thinking of leaning on him? She shook her head to clear it and raised her eyes to his.

'I can't do a thing, anyway, without…without finance.'

'It will be taken care of,' Gabriel informed her, calling for the bill and removing one of several platinum credit cards from his wallet to pay. He glanced at his watch. 'We just about have time for you to pay a visit to your office and then we will head to the house.' Back to the business in hand. For a second there he had felt a compelling need to gather the wretch up in his arms and kiss her troubled expression away. Lessons, he reminded himself harshly, are never learnt by forgetting the past.

'And don't forget,' Gabriel informed her as he pulled up just a few metres down from the estate agency, 'there is no time for any lingering farewells. I will give you five minutes.'

'Or else what?' Laura retorted, swinging open her car door and putting one long leg out of the car.

'Or else I shall come in and get you.'

And he would, too, she thought sourly as she dashed into the office. In fact, the beast would probably enjoy it. Drawing himself up to his full height, flinging his arrogant dark head back and crooking one imperious finger in her direction. In other words, bringing the entire place to a complete standstill.

She had just enough time to assure Hugo that she would call him later in the evening to explain all and to promise her work colleagues that she would keep in touch. Judging from the avidly curious expressions on their faces, she wryly thought that she would have no choice. If she didn't call them, they would make sure to call her!

She arrived back to find Gabriel standing outside, indolently leaning against the polished black driver's door of the car, and she immediately slowed her pace.

'Seven minutes,' she informed him, 'and forty-six seconds.'

'Good of me to allow you the extra two minutes and forty-six seconds, wouldn't you agree?' But he grinned wickedly when he said this and Laura felt her body surge into sudden, maddening response.

'You deserve a medal,' she muttered, hiding her confusion by sliding quickly into the car. 'What time is the surveyor coming?' she asked, once he was inside the car and gunning the engine.

'Probably there already,' Gabriel said nonchalantly.

'If not on his way back to London having got there and found no one at home.'

'Oh, Anna will wait.'

'Anna? Your chartered surveyor *is a woman*?'

'No need to sound so surprised.' Gabriel briefly slid his eyes across to her. 'This is the twenty-first century. Women have invaded the working place and many now hold down substantial jobs.'

'I know that!' Laura snapped.

'And I happen to be an extremely non-sexist employer. Everything rests on credentials, as far as I am concerned.'

Laura bit back the temptation to inform him that he could have fooled her, considering he had all the macho arrogance of someone living in another century!

'She will probably find it useful to have a look around the outside of the house and establish visually what might need doing,' he was saying now. 'She is very thorough and I trust her utterly to provide me with an unadorned statement of what will need looking at and how much I should expect to pay.'

The image of a middle-aged professional woman briskly walking around with a notepad in one hand and a pen tucked into the top pocket of her severe suit was dispersed the minute they pulled into the courtyard to find a gleaming silver Porsche parked at an angle. Before Laura could readjust her mental impression of what to expect, the woman in question rounded the corner and she wasn't wearing anything remotely resembling a severe suit. An appreciative smile curved Gabriel's lips and then he was walking towards her, arms outstretched, speaking in quick, unintelligible Spanish. And whatever he was saying, it didn't have much to do with bricks, mortar and rising damp, Laura considered sourly, lagging in the background.

At least not judging from the warm tinkle of laughter that punctuated the woman's rapid phrases.

'Laura, come and meet Anna.' He still had his arm around the other woman's waist and his mouth was still relaxed with a smile.

'This,' he said with a gesture meant to embrace the house, 'is Laura's legacy and my next purchase. What do you think?'

Close up Anna was a little older than Laura had originally surmised, but just as pretty. Small, olive-skinned, with dark eyes and dark hair that was loosely tied at the nape of her neck but with loose tendrils escaping that promised long, rebellious curls when released. And she was voluptuous. Full breasts under the tight-fitting cream jersey and tan jacket. Laura suddenly felt sick and had to force herself to smile and shake the dainty hand extended towards her.

'It needs a bit of work,' Anna was saying, all business now and commanding no less of Gabriel's attention for it. She turned to point at various bits of the house, efficiently indicating damage that Laura had not even been aware of. 'May I have a look inside?' she finished and Laura nodded curtly, leading the way whilst the other two fell back and began chatting in low tones. Low, *intimate* tones, it seemed to Laura.

She practically flung open the front door and, once in, was chagrined to be told that she could perhaps go and prepare a pot of coffee whilst the two of them made a more detailed examination of the house.

'Perhaps I ought to come along,' she suggested with saccharine sweetness. 'After all, I *have* lived in this house all my life and I would be very interested to know what repair work might have to be done.'

'No need,' Gabriel drawled. He had managed to disen-

gage himself from the raven-haired bombshell and Laura
was besieged by a further attack of acidity at the thought
that he would probably resume intimate contact the minute
they were out of sight. 'It may have been your house, but
as of tomorrow it will be in my possession. It is far more
pertinent that I find out firsthand the extent of damage.'

'I will have my report ready within a week,' Anna addressed her with a smile. 'It will be quite detailed.'

'And I'll be allowed a copy, will I?' Her voice dripped
sarcasm although Gabriel appeared blithely unaware of
that. In fact, he seemed in remarkably high spirits, Laura
thought as she politely stared him down with her hands
planted firmly on her slim hips.

'Naturally.' For sheer devilry, he once again slipped his
arm around Anna's waist before guiding her towards the
spiral staircase winding up to the first floor. God, he
wanted to look back over his shoulder just to see if she
was still standing there, all bewitching defiance, simmering. But he didn't.

In fact, he kept his arm wrapped around the brunette's
waist and only removed it when they had cleared out of
sight. And only then did he begin quizzing Anna about her
husband, Rodolfo, and their eighteen-month-old son. If his
cousin was slightly bemused by her exuberant welcome,
she concealed it well, chattering happily about family business, whilst casting her well-trained eyes into corners and
nooks and crannies and up the fireplaces for any hazards
waiting to be uncovered.

'What games are you playing, Gabriel?' she finally
asked him curiously as they inspected the last of the rooms
one and a half hours later, having agreed to call it a day.

'Games, my dearest cousin?'

'Games,' she declared firmly.

'Cat and mouse,' he said succinctly, aware that that only covered the tip of the iceberg.

'And which one is the mouse?' she teased.

'Do I resemble a mouse to you?'

'No, but then I have never seen you play this type of game with a woman before. Do not enter into something only to discover that you do not know the rules.'

'Trust me, Anna.' His eyes gleamed in anticipation of the woman waiting in the kitchen. He could feel her presence calling him. 'I am in total control...am I not always?'

CHAPTER FIVE

AN HOUR and a half spent condemned to the kitchen, side-lined into the role of onlooker in her own home, had done nothing for Laura's temper. She had usefully prepared something for herself to eat later, then had sat at the kitchen table contemplating every little thing she now thoroughly disliked about the man who had once been the centre of her life.

The fact that he was canoodling in one of the rooms with a curvaceous brunette, flaunting his sex life in front of her as a stark reminder that she was nothing to him now except a bitter taste in his mouth he was determined to eradicate, only made her more sour.

Laura remembered something her father had told her months after Gabriel had walked out of her life. She had been staring out of the kitchen window, lost in the familiar cloud of depression, when Peter Jackson had surprised her from behind. Her infernal moping around had to end, he had informed her angrily, it was not doing anyone any good at all, least of all her mother. Had she ever stopped to think, he had snapped, that she was busily mourning the loss of a man who had had his eye on the main chance? That this so-called love of her life had wanted the status and position she offered and that if she had been anyone else he would not have looked at her twice?

No, it certainly had not occurred to her then, but it was occurring to her now.

There was no shred of nostalgia in him for the past they had once shared, no hint that he remembered her wide-eyed adoration with any affection, because, she had thought in the solitude of the kitchen, he had never really cared about her.

By the time Gabriel and Anna finished their extended tour of the house, Laura was stiff-lipped with the battery of thoughts that had been whirling around in her head.

She stood up when she heard their footsteps, arms folded. And he *still* had his infernal arm around the woman's waist!

'Something smells good in here,' Gabriel said, disengaging himself. 'Anna, you'll stay for some coffee, won't you?' Her body language was speaking volumes, he thought with satisfaction. Arms folded, face rigid with disapproval. Yes, he was utterly and pleasurably in control. The thought did wonders for his sense of well-being.

'I can't, Gabriel.' The brunette smiled apologetically. 'It's late and I face a long drive back to London.' She gave him a look of intimate and indulgent affection that had Laura's teeth snapping together.

'What is the state of the house?' she asked with freezing politeness. 'Mr Greppi seems to think that it's on the verge of collapsing.' *Gabriel?* Did he really expect her to believe that all his employees addressed him by his first name in tones of warm intimacy? He might see himself as Mr Ultra Modern Man with his staff, but did that stance include running his hands all over their bodies in full view of whoever might be watching? If so, then she was surprised he didn't spend half his time in a court somewhere fighting off harassment suits. Not that this particular woman looked in the least upset by his intentions!

'Far from it,' Anna said warmly, collecting her bag and briefcase from the counter. 'There's nothing fundamentally wrong with your house.'

'*My* house,' Gabriel corrected, shooting Laura a rueful

smile that the correction had to be made, one that she countered with icy blankness.

Anna shook her head and said something in Spanish, then she turned to Laura. 'My report should be ready within a week, but there really will be no need for any extensive repair work. The window sills need looking after. Some of them have rotted through, and I noticed that some small parts of the roof will need replacing, but aside from that any damage is superficial. Years of neglect take their toll.'

'Yes, I realise that.'

'Now, now, there is no need to sound so offended,' Gabriel mocked. 'Anna is just doing her job. Now, perhaps you could get that coffee ready whilst I see Anna out?'

'If I'm going to be working for you, then we need to get a few things straight,' was the first thing Laura told him when he reappeared in the kitchen a few minutes later.

She had taken up residence by the kitchen table, but even with the distance between them she was still agonisingly aware of his suffocating masculinity. Especially now that there was no third party around to dilute it.

'Ah, coffee. Just what I need.' He picked up the mug, took a sip and then moved in her direction, making sure that he passed fractionally too close to her before pulling out one of the chairs and sitting down.

He wasn't wearing a tie, but he undid the top two buttons of his shirt, tugging open the neck and running his long brown fingers along the underside of the fabric whilst Laura watched in helpless fascination, before dragging her mind back to the grievances she had rehearsed.

'Point one,' she informed him, 'is that I'm not your servant. Don't think that when you happen to be around you can snap your fingers and I'll run and make you, and whoever else happens to be with you, a cup of coffee.'

Gabriel looked at her lazily whilst he continued to slowly sip his coffee. He wondered whether he should just inform her that really she did not have much option when it came to her list of duties, and then decided that constant confrontation was not going to achieve what was becoming increasingly important. Namely, her. In bed with him. Wet, willing and naked.

He was the cat, yes, and admittedly she was the mouse, but she would be oh, such a very eager mouse when she came to him.

He smiled at the thought of that, which was disconcerting enough to make Laura stop in her tracks. She had expected him to jump in with another little reminder of her indebtedness to him, which included making however many cups of coffee he wanted. In fact, she had prepared quite a good argument to counteract any objections. What she hadn't expected was for him to smile, a slow, gleaming smile that sent a shiver of treacherous awareness rippling through her.

'You are absolutely right,' he said, maintaining his killer smile.

'I am?'

He nodded.

'Yes, of course I'm right. I don't intend to be used, Gabriel, or to do any running and fetching for you.' She could hear herself blustering but then, dammit, did he have to sit there and look so damned agreeable?

'I would not expect you to. Indeed, if I gave you the impression that I was...throwing my weight around, then I apologise. Profusely.' He could fully understand why she was staring at him with such suspicious incomprehension. He had done nothing *but* throw his weight around since he had set eyes on her again, and it wasn't going to do. He didn't want her cowed and spitting hate at him. He wanted her sweet and compliant and deliciously abandoned.

Besides, what was the good of rejecting someone who viewed him with intense dislike? It would amount to no rejection. For the second time, she would simply be relieved to see the back of him. She might be aware of him, in fact *was* aware of him…he could feel it in those hot little surreptitious glances she occasionally slid across to him when she wasn't aware that he was looking…but as long as he continued to wield the rod of power, she would resolutely fight the attraction with every ounce of strength.

Sure, he wanted to remind her at every turn that she was now dependent on him, but every little reminder only drove her that bit further away. Only a fool sabotaged his own game plan with pointless hollow victories.

'Oh,' Laura said, taken aback.

'What were those other points of yours you wanted to mention?'

'Nothing,' she mumbled, gulping down the remainder of her coffee. 'Well…' She looked outside at the darkness that had fallen and wrapped itself around the house. 'It's getting late. Perhaps you should be setting off…'

Gabriel could see her tense in anticipation of another confrontation and so he obligingly got to his feet.

'You're right.'

Laura felt that she should be breathing a heartfelt sigh of relief. Why then did she feel just a little bit disappointed at the speed with which he had taken her up on her suggestion? Surely she didn't *want* him to hang around any longer? That would be downright masochistic!

'It will take me at least an hour and a half to get back,' he chatted casually as he headed out of the kitchen and towards the front door. He would have liked to have given her something to think about after he had gone, a light kiss somewhere innocent yet deeply arousing, perhaps on the side of her neck. Nothing that would indicate the desire for anything else. But there was no point in barging through the sudden window he had created for himself.

Having been so thoroughly wrong-footed, Laura was now overcome by an attack of guilt. It was already after eight and she had offered him nothing to eat. She should at least have suggested that he share the economical dinner she had made for herself. In fact, she had opened her mouth to offer the invitation when caution made her stifle back the words.

'So tomorrow,' he said, turning around to face her, 'perhaps you could meet me at your accountant's office?' Her slightly flushed face and half-parted lips were appealing enough to almost make him forget his resolve not to frighten her away. That mouth was begging to be plundered. His hands ached from wanting to plunge into that prim top of hers and expose the soft, heavy breasts with their tempting, pert nipples. He stuck his hands severely into his pockets.

'What time?'

'Nine-thirty. He will be expecting us. My fax confirming the purchase as well as all the contracts with stipulations should have reached him some time this afternoon. In case I failed to mention it, you and I will have to agree on a price for the furniture contained in the house. At least, those items of furniture you wish to sell, of course. Naturally, you can keep the rest here until such time as you wish to remove them.'

'You mean when you're ready for me to move out?' She saw that he had flushed darkly at her words and wondered whether he was perhaps not immune to the slightest twinge of guilt that he was going to be throwing her out of the only house she had ever lived in.

Did she realise, Gabriel wondered, what a vision of temptation she presented when she dropped her guard? He couldn't help it but he could see the swell of her breasts and his torrid imagination made him flush. 'There is no rush for you to contemplate any such move,' he said briefly, turning to open the door just in case he did something he regretted. 'This is not an ordinary house purchase. You will be in charge of running this show and the best place for you to be will be right here, for obvious reasons. But we can discuss all of this tomorrow.'

'Right. Yes. Of course.' Perfectly businesslike. Obviously he no longer felt the need to remind her at every turn that he was the one in the position of doing her a favour. In fact, he obviously no longer felt the need to dwell at all on the fact that they weren't strangers. He was a businessman first and foremost and this had all now become business.

Laura waited by the open doorway, watching as he strode towards his car, got in and began driving carefully out of the courtyard and down towards the road at the bottom of the long drive.

Now that he had gone, the house seemed suddenly very empty. She ate her meal to the deafening sound of silence and went to bed thinking unwelcome thoughts of Gabriel and the Porsche-driving chartered surveyor with the easy smile and the darkly sexy body. They made a stunning match. Both olive-skinned, both raven-haired, both obviously at ease in each other's company.

Not that Gabriel and his love life were any concern of hers, she told herself firmly the following morning as she made her way to Phillip Carr's office in the centre of town.

She had half expected him to arrive late, but in fact he was already there by the time she was shown into Phillip's office, sitting with his back to her, relaxed and confident.

'I've been looking through the papers,' Phillip greeted her warmly, delighted with the solution to a problem over which he had been regularly losing sleep. 'Everything seems to be in order. In fact, Mr Greppi has been most meticulous in his attention to detail.'

Gabriel was smiling at the older man, receiving the compliment with nonchalant modesty, but out of the corner of his eye he was vibrantly aware of Laura slipping into the chair alongside his. Her pale hair gleamed like silk and he approved of what she was wearing. A short-sleeved rose-coloured dress that was simple but fitted, emphasising the narrowness of her waist and the length of her legs, which seemed to go on for ever. Despite what he had said about her losing weight, there was no chance she would ever be mistaken for one of those stick-thin models, two of whom he had dated in the past and neither of whom had done much for him. Her body was a bit more streamlined than it had been seven years ago but she was too full-breasted to ever look skinny. And she still had the athletic firmness of someone accustomed to an outdoor life. He slid his eyes away and began to pay more attention to Phillip, who was now going over some of the details of the contract with his client.

When he got to the part about her salary, Laura gave a little squeak of astonishment, rapidly followed by an objection.

'No way,' she said firmly, turning to face Gabriel for the first time since she had entered the room. He was dressed for work and looked no less impressive for it. Dark charcoal-grey suit, crisp white shirt, dark blue tie with a small, clever pattern running through it. He swung his chair to look directly at her, one eyebrow raised in apparent enquiry.

'No way...what?' he asked, sitting back and lightly linking his fingers on his lap.

'Phillip, would you mind giving Gabriel and myself a few minutes of privacy?'

'Is that really necessary, Laura?' Phillip asked. 'I honestly cannot see what the problem is here and the sooner we go through this contract, the sooner we can have the deal signed, sealed and delivered, so to speak.' Before, he added to himself, our knight in shining armour decides to have a change of heart. Everything, so far, looked too good to be true and in Phillip's experience canny businessmen rarely indulged in deals that were too good to be true. Not unless they were the eventual winners, which certainly was not the case here. He tried to signal as much to Laura with his eyes but she was steadfastly ignoring him and, with a click of his tongue, he reluctantly stood up.

'So,' Gabriel said, pushing his chair back so that he could cross his long legs, ankle resting on knee, fingers still linked on his lap as he lightly rubbed the pads of his thumbs together, 'what is the problem here? I confess I'm baffled.' He tilted his head to one side and devoted every nerve in his body to looking at her.

'Baffled!' Laura gave a snort of disbelief. 'Oh, please. I know exactly what you're doing here, Gabriel. Overpaying me so that I'm even more indebted to you than I already am! You're offering to give me *five times* more than I was getting working for Hugo, and that's when I was working *full-time* there!'

He shook his head. 'This is a record. The first time anyone has attacked me for *overpaying* them!'

'You mean you've been attacked for *underpaying*?' Laura smirked, distracted.

'No...actually, I usually manage to get it just right.'

'Mr Perfect Employer. I wonder why I'm not surprised

to hear you singing your own praises. Could it be that I'm getting accustomed to your ego, which is as big as a house?'

'I am Argentinian! You insult my pride...' But he grinned when he said this and Laura found herself grinning back, caught up in a moment of perfect wry and mutual understanding. Until she remembered the matter at hand.

'Anyway, you're distracting me...'

'Oh, good,' Gabriel murmured wickedly, 'success at last.'

Which brought a bright flare of colour to her cheeks as the velvety ambiguity of his words struck home. 'I *mean* you're distracting me from what I was saying. Which is that there's no need to be so ridiculously generous. It's enough,' she continued, taking a deep breath, 'that you're buying the riding stables, that you're going to try and turn it around, that you've offered me this lifeline.' Laura lowered her eyes. 'And in case I haven't said this before...thank you.'

'What was that?' He leaned forward, cupping one ear with his hand.

'You heard me.' A small smile tugged the corners of her mouth.

'Accept my generosity,' Gabriel said, holding onto her softening and feeling something tug deep inside him. 'There is nothing self-serving about it. The job will be a big one. I am merely compensating you in a manner I judge fit.' He gave her a crooked smile. 'Please.'

'You should at least give me a probationary period,' Laura offered. 'You may not approve of the way I handle things...'

'Why not?' He raised his eyebrows in lazy amusement. 'Are you planning on going down a few illegal routes? A spot of bribery or blackmail? Sleeping with a few contacts to generate business?'

'Of course not!' Laura flushed. 'I would never dream of doing anything of the sort!'

'You mean the bribery and blackmail or the sleeping with contacts…?'

'Both! All! You know what I mean.'

'Then I see no reason why you should be on any probationary period, but…' he shrugged '…if it makes you happy then we can agree on a three-month probation.'

'During which you would expect me to achieve…what? Precisely?'

'Why don't we discuss that later? In the meanwhile, we might just as well get Phillip back in so that we can finish here. I take it your little argument over pay is sorted…'

'I suppose so,' Laura said limply.

The remainder of the meeting, which lasted a full two and a half hours with only the odd snatched break for some coffee and biscuits, moved at a dizzying speed. Sums of money were thrown around that made her gasp. Guided by Phillip, she signed on the various dotted lines he indicated, barely aware of the various contracts she was reading. By the time she and Gabriel were shown out of the office, Laura felt as though she were unsteadily coming off a roller-coaster ride.

The fish, Gabriel thought as he followed her out onto the pavement, was on the hook. All he had to do now was enjoy the unparalleled experience of reeling it in. And reel it in he would. With every signature, he had been grimly aware of the fortuitous sequence of events that had brought him to this point. He now owned the house that had once been barred from the likes of him, and in a manner of speaking, whether it was politically correct or not to even think it, he owned the woman who had once casually and cruelly turned him away. Or perhaps he didn't own her, he thought with brutal honesty. But he would.

'Are you heading back down to London now?' Laura asked, breaking into his thoughts. 'I suppose it's been difficult for you to find the time to keep coming up here.'

He noticed that she was heading towards her car, the old relic of a Land Rover her father used to drive, and which she had presumably been obliged to continue using because of her straitened financial circumstances.

'That car will have to go,' he said abruptly.

Laura stopped in her tracks and looked at him with her mouth open. 'I beg your pardon?'

'The car. It will have to go.'

'What do you mean *the car will have to go*? That car works perfectly well. Well-ish, anyway. And in case you hadn't noticed, I don't have a replacement waiting in the wings. Besides, it's very sturdy, which is what I need living where I do.' Laura began walking towards it, trying hard not to notice the rust spreading along the bottom of the driver's door.

'It won't do.' Gabriel swept his eyes over the denim-blue vehicle with an expression of disdain.

'Is this part of your continuing plan to strip me of everything?' Laura flared up at him angrily.

The accusation was so close to the truth that Gabriel had the decency to blush, but he stood his ground, his mouth thinning in determination. 'It is no such thing. I simply feel that your driving around in that heap of crumbling metal is not exactly going to give any prospective clients the right impression of a business on the road to recovery.'

They stared at one another until Laura helplessly lowered her eyes. 'I can't just go out and buy another car,' she protested stubbornly.

'Why not?'

'Because…'

'Our business here has not been completed. We are about to pay a little visit to the local bank where I will set up a substantial account for you from which you will withdraw whatever money is necessary to cover costs. Your salary will be transferred directly into the bank account you now possess.' He looked at the mutinous set of her mouth and shook his head. 'There is no point in trying to fight me every inch of the way,' he informed her softly. 'You will never win.'

'No,' Laura jeered, 'because you're bigger and stronger and infinitely richer. Am I on the right track here?'

'Pretty much.' He shrugged.

'You can set up bank accounts, snap your fingers and make me do your bidding, force me to part with just about the only thing I possess to my name now that the house has gone.'

'The house but not the contents,' he reminded her. 'And you still have the clothes you wear.'

'Which you will doubtless decide to make me get rid of somewhere along the way?' His failure to answer, in fact to look as though her jabbing attack had even remotely dented his formidable self-composure, was added fuel to the fire. 'I may obey you,' Laura said through gritted teeth, 'and I may be grateful for everything you've done, but I'll never like you.'

His only reaction was the tiny pulsing muscle in his jaw, an indication that her words were getting to him.

He would not rise to her bait. She could glower until the cows came home, Gabriel thought, but to no purpose because he was not going to indulge in a heated argument with her.

Besides, in a strange way, he knew how she was feeling.

He knew that her anger stemmed from her helplessness, from her sudden vulnerability. When she'd still had the house and the land and the decrepit sign announcing the riding stables that were no more, she'd still felt, psychologically, that she'd still had *something*. That ownership had passed to him, of all people, was therefore more than galling.

The sudden, startling insight into the woman fulminating not five inches away from him aroused a compassion he had no time for.

'Let us go to the bank,' he said in a tight voice.

'I want to go home.'

'I know you do,' Gabriel said gently. But then his face hardened. 'And you will. Just as soon as we have sorted out our finances.'

An implacable wall, Laura thought. She could rail and storm and beat her fists against it, but it would never budge. Her shoulders drooped and she nodded in resignation.

'And then,' he announced with supreme arrogance as they walked the short distance to the bank, 'we will go and buy you a car.'

The bank manager, who miraculously seemed to have a huge window in his day in order to jump to Gabriel's commands, was as fawning and beaming as Phillip had been.

'You,' Laura said sarcastically, during the five-minute pause in the conversation during which the impressionable and youthful bank manager had seen fit to rush off and order his secretary to halt all his calls until otherwise told, 'are obviously the most exciting thing that has happened to Tony Jenkins this year. If he bends over backwards any more, I think the back of his head will touch the ground.'

Gabriel looked at her appreciatively and grinned. He had

forgotten how damned funny she could be when she tried. 'Perhaps he is impressed by my good looks and winning personality,' he commented drily.

'Perhaps he's even more impressed by all those numbers you're giving him.'

'Shallow man,' Gabriel murmured in a low voice, his dark eyes making her go hot all over. 'Someone should tell him that money is not everything.'

'I hate it when people quote me.' But she looked away quickly and was inordinately relieved when the subject of their discussion reappeared.

'And now,' Gabriel said as soon as they had stepped outside, Laura now in possession of so much money with which to commence this venture that her head was spinning, 'for the car.'

'There's no need for that just yet, is there?' she said, trailing powerlessly along behind him, reluctantly impressed by the awesome business acumen he had displayed over the past few hours. 'I mean,' she continued breathlessly as she walked quickly to keep up with his easy, purposeful stride, 'I can sort of look around in the next few weeks...'

'I have always found that it is best to strike whilst the iron is hot.'

'And what if *I* don't want to strike!'

Gabriel paused to look at her. God, but he was enjoying himself. In fact, he didn't think that he had enjoyed a morning's work quite as much as he had today. He had almost forgotten his long-term plan, the stakes he had begun planting that would reap their own reward, namely her acquiescence. When she stopped fighting him, he could almost begin to recapture that heady, pleasurable and utterly treacherous attraction he had felt for her. An attraction that went far beyond the physical.

It was a mistake he was not about to make.

'Then, naturally, I will respect your wishes,' he said smoothly.

'As you would any of your employees'?'

'I always listen to what others say,' Gabriel confirmed ambiguously. 'If you want to have a breather before you begin looking for a car, then by all means.' He glanced down at his watch. 'In fact, it is almost time for lunch. Why don't we go somewhere and have a bite to eat? Mmm?'

Laura suddenly and inexplicably felt the sharp edge of panic rip through her. The sun was bright and hard and emphasised every angle of his face. And what she saw disturbed her. More than that, frightened her.

'Don't you have to get back to London?' she asked nervously. He had an empire to run, for heaven's sake! Surely he couldn't spend all his time swanning around up here in the manner of a country squire with nothing better to do?

As if he had read her mind, he said wryly, 'I am the boss. I can come and go as I please and there is still too much to do here for me to leave at the moment.' But she was right. Sophisticated though communications were, he still needed to be physically present in his office some time soon and once there he would find himself bombarded with all the minutiae that he had hitherto enjoyed but which would take his mind off the business in hand.

He would have to speed things along.

He gave her a shuttered look. 'What about that little Italian just at the corner over there?' Very deliberately he placed his hand on the small of her back, and even though he felt her tense under the slight pressure of his touch, he didn't remove it. In fact, his contact widened until he was guiding her across the road with his hand circling her waist.

A purely routine gesture, Laura thought frantically. They had just completed a huge deal by any standards and he was probably just trying to show some sign of friendliness. It was her fault if her body was reacting like dry tinder being set ablaze. He had a girlfriend already anyway. The thought of that steadied her and as soon as they had crossed the road she politely pulled out of his grasp.

They could carry on like this for ever, Gabriel thought suddenly. One small move on his part followed by five large steps back on hers. She had been warned off him from the start and any ceasefire between them was doomed to falter.

He snapped his teeth together in angry impatience. Biding time was all well and good but it wasn't his style. By tonight, he promised himself. He would taste those lips by the end of the evening and then he would begin his assault on her senses.

'Tell me,' he said as soon as they were shown to a table, 'what is the state of your love life?'

'What?' Flabbergasted, Laura looked at him in pure amazement.

'Your love life,' Gabriel repeated. 'What is the state of it? By which I mean, do you have a lover?'

'I know what you mean! I was just stupefied that you have the nerve to ask!'

'Well, I do,' he said calmly.

'It's none of your business.'

'I wish I could be as phlegmatic about it as you are...' He paused and Laura felt an unnerving tug of anticipation as she wondered feverishly where he was going with this one. Would he be jealous if she *did* have a lover? He had always had a jealous streak a mile wide and she couldn't stop the sizzle of intense excitement at the thought of

GET FREE BOOKS and a FREE GIFT WHEN YOU PLAY THE...

Just scratch off the silver box with a coin. Then check below to see the gifts you get!

SLOT MACHINE GAME!

YES! I have scratched off the silver box. Please send me the 2 free Harlequin Presents® books and gift for which I qualify. I understand I am under no obligation to purchase any books, as explained on the back of this card.

306 HDL DRRK

106 HDL DRRZ
(H-P-01/03)

FIRST NAME	LAST NAME

ADDRESS

APT.#	CITY

STATE/PROV.	ZIP/POSTAL CODE

7	7	7
🍒	🍒	🍒
♣	♣	♣
🔔	🔔	🔔

7 7 7 Worth TWO FREE BOOKS plus a BONUS Mystery Gift!

Worth TWO FREE BOOKS!

Worth ONE FREE BOOK!

TRY AGAIN!

Visit us online at www.eHarlequin.com

DETACH AND MAIL CARD TODAY!

The Harlequin Reader Service® — Here's how it works:

Accepting your 2 free books and gift places you under no obligation to buy anything. You may keep the books and gift and return the shipping statement marked "cancel." If you do not cancel, about a month later we'll send you 6 additional books and bill you just $3.57 each in the U.S., or $4.24 each in Canada, plus 25¢ shipping & handling per book and applicable taxes if any.* That's the complete price and — compared to cover prices of $4.25 each in the U.S. and $4.99 each in Canada — it's quite a bargain! You may cancel at any time, but if you choose to continue, every month we'll send you 6 more books, which you may either purchase at the discount price or return to us and cancel your subscription.

*Terms and prices subject to change without notice. Sales tax applicable in N.Y. Canadian residents will be charged applicable provincial taxes and GST.

arousing his jealousy now, ridiculous though any such notion might be.

'But it makes sense for me to know, as your employer. If you were...involved with a man, I would obviously try and curtail too many trips that necessitate overnight stays... Oh, come on, Laura, it is a purely practical question.' Dark eyes lazily inspected her face.

'I...well, at the moment, I'm not actually involved with anyone, so I would be free to overnight anywhere should the situation require it. Not that that was really any business of yours. I mean, I don't ask *you* about Anna, do I?'

'Anna?' For a few seconds he had no idea what she was talking about.

'Oh, don't pretend to be all innocence, Gabriel.' Let him say it, she thought viciously. Then this unwanted pull of attraction will go away under the burden of reality. 'You know who I mean. The dusky bombshell you were cuddling up to at the house. I believe she goes under the title of your chartered surveyor!'

'Oh, *that* Anna.' He smiled slowly and positively purred with the satisfaction of having drawn her out into the open. 'My cousin.'

The game was on. He was back in full control and ready to pounce.

CHAPTER SIX

'YOUR cousin.' Laura tried to give a snort of disbelieving laughter, but she was rapidly reaching the conclusion, the mortifying conclusion, that he was telling the truth. 'Ha,' she finished weakly.

'You didn't think...no, surely not!' Gabriel leaned closer to her. 'I am shocked!'

He didn't look shocked. In fact, he looked remarkably pleased with himself. Without too much effort, Laura could quite easily have hit him over the head with something very hard. Instead, she composed herself and stared at him haughtily. The man was playing games with her, which was bad enough. Worse, though, was the fact that, instead of her feeling insulted and outraged, the wicked glitter in those black eyes was shooting to the very heart of her, making her skin burn.

'Men *do* have affairs with women who work with them. Or *for* them. It's not unheard of.'

'Ah, you do not give me sufficient credit.' He sat back and continued staring at her as a waitress approached their table and took their orders of lasagne, which was the first thing that came to Laura's head and Gabriel, without glancing at the menu, fell in line. All the better, she thought sourly, to get rid of the waitress so that he could continue his little pretence of nursing wounded feelings.

'I have always made it a policy of mine never to get sexually involved with a member of staff,' he said piously. 'It can lead to all sorts of complications.' He hoped she wouldn't remember that when she was lying, spent and fulfilled, in his arms.

'There's no need to explain yourself to me,' Laura mumbled ungraciously.

'Anna and I have always been close. When she came to England to study and qualified as a chartered surveyor, I was delighted to be able to offer her a job with the company. In fact,' he said confidentially, 'I am godfather to her little boy.'

'Lovely,' Laura said.

There was a fractional silence, during which she was intensely aware of him looking at her whilst she gazed down in apparent fascination at the tips of her fingers resting on the table.

'You weren't...' he allowed the pause to drag on until she reluctantly raised her eyes to his '...*jealous*, were you?'

'Of course I wasn't jealous!' Laura scoffed. 'Why on earth should I be?'

Gabriel spread his hands in a flamboyantly Latin American gesture of bafflement.

'I don't have any claims over you, Gabriel, any more than you have over me. Yes, we were involved a long time ago. And yes, we're involved now, but in a completely different way. This time, it's all about business. You're now my paymaster.'

He didn't like that. Not one little bit. She could see it in the immediate narrowing of his eyes.

'I do not care for that term *paymaster*.'

Laura shrugged. 'It's the truth. You now are the lord and master of what used to be my home and you are perfectly entitled to bring anyone there you want to. You could bring an entire harem of women!'

She could feel him positively fulminating as they ate their lunch in virtual silence.

This was not how Gabriel had envisaged their conversation going. With every short, blunt, factual observation she had managed to distance herself from him in a way nothing he could say would have succeeded in doing. Now, as he broodingly cast his eyes on her face, down-turned as she half-heartedly toyed with some food at the end of her fork, as if debating whether or not she should eat any more, he could sense her getting more and more remote.

She was drawing lines between them and he knew that, once those lines were drawn, she would set them in cement. And, God, he didn't want her behind any lines. He couldn't understand it, but the threat of her remoteness was wreaking havoc with his composure.

He pushed aside his half-finished oval plate of food and sat back in the chair, watching her as she made sure not to look at him.

'Is it not ironic that we are doing now what we should have done all those years ago?' he asked softly, and she raised startled eyes to his.

'What's that?'

'Sharing a meal.'

'I told you, circumstances have changed.' She went back to her labours with the food whilst inside her giddy little leaps were taking place.

'You asked me before how it was that I had never married. Let me ask you now, how is it that *you* never married?'

Laura shrugged.

'What does that...' he imitated her shrug '...mean?'

'It means that the opportunity never arose.' She couldn't stomach another mouthful. 'What would you like me to

begin with first, Gabriel? I mean, should I concentrate on
fixing up meetings with people to try and regain business,
or should I start working on the land to bring it up to
scratch? You need to give me my list of duties so that I
can—'

'Dammit, woman!' Gabriel exploded. 'Would you stop
behaving as though you're…you're…?' For the first time
since he could remember, his cool power of articulate
speech deserted him completely.

'Your employee?' Laura said helpfully. 'But that's exactly what I am.'

'There is no need for you to put on this ridiculous act
of bowing and scraping!' he growled, realising that she
had somehow managed to get him into a corner. How, he
had no idea.

'I'm not bowing and scraping. I'm asking you to define
my duties in order of importance. Besides, I would have
thought that it might have made your day to have me bowing and scraping.'

It damned well should have done, Gabriel thought ruefully. When he had picked up that newspaper and read
about the riding stables, it had certainly been top of his
aims to see the wretch in a position where the tables had
been reversed.

Somewhere along the way, things had changed. He most
certainly did not want to see her bowing and scraping.

'Well, you are wrong,' he told her brusquely. 'If you
want me to tell you what I expect from you, then I will,
but I would prefer that we discuss it together.'

'You mean pretend that this is a normal situation and
that you haven't just bought me out lock, stock and barrel
for the sole purpose of getting your own back?'

'Dammit, Laura…'

'I'm sorry. I'm just a little edgy because this deal has

now been done and I've become a lodger in my own house, on my own land.'

'You would have been in that situation anyway,' Gabriel pointed out darkly. 'The place had to be sold and chances are you would have got a lot less on the open market. And you would not have been living there. You would now be out searching for somewhere you could afford.' He couldn't bear the trace of sadness in her eyes even though he was honest enough to realise that he had been instrumental in putting it there. She didn't see him as her rescuer, she saw him as her gaoler and it was like a knife twisting slowly in his gut.

'I know.'

'Then stop punishing me for offering you a good deal. And you are not a lodger in your own home, dammit, Laura. You belong there and you are to look on it as yours.'

'But it's not, is it?'

Gabriel counted very slowly in Spanish to ten. 'Okay. I think we ought to concentrate on getting the house into a good condition first of all. It's going to be the least time-consuming of the tasks and the most immediately rewarding. So what about we leave this place, head back to the house and then we can have a look around and decide what is to be done? And if you tell me that it's up to me because I am now the owner, then I will personally throttle you.'

'Oh, I'm quivering with fear, Gabriel.' But the fight had gone out of her voice. She could feel him tiptoeing his way towards her, trying to make her see his point of view, and his sudden vulnerability was more moving than any of his aggressive thrusts at her had been. She raised her eyebrows in amusement and he offered her a crooked smile in return.

'Good. That's more like it.'

'Oh, you approve of women quivering in fear, do you?'

He looked at her for so long and in such concentrated silence that she became aware of the subtle change in the atmosphere. From combatants to ex-lovers. The intangible electricity made her flesh crawl and Laura lowered her eyes quickly.

'Let's get out of here.' He beckoned for the bill, paid it and then stood up.

All through the drive back to the house he made polite, surface conversation, asking her what improvements she would like for the house, but the undercurrent between them still rose and fell, until by the time he screeched to a halt outside the house he thought he would pass out from wanting to touch her.

So much for the master seducer, he thought ruefully. He couldn't wait to leap out of the car so that he could try and clear his head. Whilst she...she seemed utterly in control, barely speaking, occasionally glancing out of the window with a thoughtful expression on her face, which made him want to stop the car immediately and demand to know what she was thinking.

'Shall we have a look straight away?' Laura asked as soon as they were in the hall. 'If I know what you want, then I can get going first thing in the morning.'

Gabriel gritted his teeth together in frustration and watched as she kicked off her formal shoes so that she was now barefoot.

'Let's start with downstairs.'

'I'll just go and fetch some paper.'

'Oh, for God's sake, is that really necessary, Laura?'

'It'll help me remember if I just jot down what you say.' Their eyes clashed for a few seconds, and then she fled to the kitchen where she dug around until she managed to excavate a sheet of A4 paper and a pen.

This was proving to be even harder than she could ever have dreamt in a million years. If she could have held onto her hostility. If he could just have done her the favour of remaining a one-dimensional cardboard cut-out—ex-lover with an axe to grind. But no, he had to turn things on their head, he had to be gentle and amusing one minute only to switch back into arrogant aggression.

She returned to find him in the sitting room, staring around him. 'I came here that last day to see your parents. Did you know that?' Gabriel had not meant to utter a word about that fateful, humiliating episode, but now that he had he could see that he had shocked her.

'You came *here*?' She shook her head in bewilderment. 'Whatever for?'

'To ask for your hand in marriage.' His mouth twisted cynically and he continued to watch her face as it was suffused with colour. 'Naturally I was thrown out on my ears.'

'I didn't know.'

'No. I did not expect your papa to confide that little titbit to you.'

'He didn't dislike you, Gabriel, he just thought…'

'That his baby could do better?'

'Isn't that what all fathers think?' Her eyes flashed suddenly. 'If *you* had a young daughter and the situation was the same, wouldn't *you* have reacted in exactly the same way?'

'Naturally not,' Gabriel said shortly, but her retort had him turning away. 'Anyway, it is all water under the bridge. For the moment, we have other things to talk about.'

'You're the one who raised the subject.'

'It's history. Tell me what you suggest for this room. I find it too dark and depressing.'

'It's your house,' Laura said stubbornly, and he shot her a glowering look from under his lashes.

'And I am ordering you to tell me what you think.'

'I like greens,' she said finally, when the option was either to say what she thought or remain locked in silence, which she knew he had no intention of breaking. 'And creams. Autumnal colours. Mum liked all this floral stuff and when she became, well, really ill, she said it cheered her up to look at the flowers on the walls.' Laura's mouth trembled and she frowned down at the piece of paper in her hand.

'I'm sorry.'

She had barely noticed how close he had come to her. He filled her nostrils with his masculine scent.

'You can cry, *querida*. Tears are nothing to be ashamed of.'

'Of course I'm not going to cry.' She shook her head briskly and looked up at him. It was the gentle compassion in his eyes that did it. She blinked and felt the hot sting of tears begin to seep from under her eyelids, and suddenly his arms were around her, pulling her towards him.

Laura allowed herself to be folded against his broad chest. She hooked her arms around his waist and he seemed to just wrap himself around her, one hand on her back, the other pressed against the side of her head, whilst his fingers weaved through her hair. She could hear him making soothing noises under his breath, which only made matters worse because the oozing of her tears became more of a torrent until her body was shaking from crying.

Eventually, she edged herself away, only conscious now of how closely their bodies had been entwined, and raised her eyes to his.

'I'm very sorry. Not very professional.' She tried to give

a self-deprecating laugh, which emerged as a croak of sorts.

'Here.' He reached into his pocket and handed her a handkerchief, which Laura gratefully accepted, but he continued holding her tightly against him. It felt good. Better than good, he thought.

'I'm fine now,' she said in a more normal voice.

'Sure?' Gabriel tilted her face with one finger under her chin and then softly brushed away the remainder of dampness on her cheeks with the pad of his thumb.

'Sure. Thanks for the hankie. I'll wash it and return it to you.' She had to remove herself from this clinch. Her breasts were pushed against his chest and, now that she was no longer sobbing like a maiden in distress, she was all too aware of them reacting with perky vigour to his body. As was the rest of her. Where his fingers had traced her cheekbones, her skin burned. She wanted to just tiptoe and capture that beautiful, arrogant mouth with hers. She wanted to close her eyes and lose herself in him.

She made a concerted effort to draw back and succeeded.

'I'm not sure what came over me,' she apologised with a watery smile.

'Memories,' Gabriel said gruffly, sticking his hands into his pockets. A perfect opportunity missed, he thought regretfully. He was definitely losing his touch. He had had her there, in his arms, as vulnerable as a newborn babe and, instead of seizing the opportunity, he had played the understanding gentleman, had *wanted* to play the understanding gentleman. He wondered whether years of being the object of pursuit had dulled his talent for the chase.

'The room could certainly do with an overhaul, though,' Laura said, moving away. 'What would *you* like to see here? I...' She sighed and frowned. 'The furniture will look odd if the room is done up around it. Old-fashioned.'

'Then sell it, Laura. Put the proceeds into your bank account.'

For when I'm thrown off the premises, she thought. Because she had no doubt that off the premises was exactly where she was heading, despite all his talk about treating his house as hers. Nor would she allow three seconds of sympathy to get to her and make her forget that their relationship now was just precisely what she had told him, namely a business arrangement.

Her eyes skittered across to him and she licked her lips.

'Why don't I just leave you in charge of the decorating?' he suggested.

'Because I don't know the first thing about interior design. And I wouldn't feel comfortable...taking charge of somewhere that's not my own.'

'Oh, God. Here we go again.'

'No, really, Gabriel. I'm not about to start...'

'Reminding me that I'm the big, bad wolf who has deprived you of your family home?'

Instead of rushing headlong into defending her position, Laura smiled sheepishly. 'Right. What I'm saying is that I'm not exactly...you know, the height of fashion...' She could feel every word turning into a tongue-twister as he stood stock-still and regarded her with that dark, disturbingly penetrating look of his that made her toes curl.

'The height of fashion...? What has fashion got to do with anything?'

'A lot. It has a lot to do with...I mean, Gabriel, look at you and look at me.' He duly cast his eyes down his body then ran his eyes over hers, paying a lot more attention to every inch of her. When he finally met her eyes, she was blushing furiously.

'Yes, there are some obvious differences but I would put those down to gender.' He raised one eyebrow in amusement and Laura remained staunchly unmoved by the provocatively inviting glitter in his eyes.

'You want the best. It's obvious from the way you dress, Gabriel. I…I've led an outdoor life and never had much time for how I looked.'

'Where are we going with this one?'

'I don't know anything about furnishing a house to the sort of standard a man like you would expect!'

'A man like me…' Gabriel mused coolly. 'You forget that I did not always possess this wealth.'

'And now you do,' Laura persisted stubbornly, 'and I'm sure you would want furnishings that reflect your…your status.'

'Oh, naturally,' he mocked, 'I could not possibly want somewhere comfortable and soothing when I could have something very expensive and probably very ostentatious. I do not intend to make this a permanent base, but when I do come here, I assure you I will not be looking to surround myself with heavy velvet drapes and silk on the walls. Nor will I want the taps to be gold-plated.'

'Why do you always have to jump to the other extreme?'

'Why do you always have to pigeon-hole? If you do not feel confident about decorating this place, then feel free to hire an interior designer.' He shrugged, as if suddenly bored by the conversation. He didn't want to be here discussing wall colours and furniture requirements, he thought suddenly. As long as they continued trawling from room to room with Laura clutching that stupid sheet of paper, they would remain on opposite sides of an insurmountable wall. He, the boss in charge, she the employee who had been bailed out. And it didn't matter one jot if her eyes kept sliding over to him of their own accord. She would keep her instincts at bay and listen to her head.

'Is that what you did with your own house? Hired an interior designer?'

'I have no time to sit in shops poring over wallpaper books and shopping for little artefacts. I gave my designer free rein and she did the rest.'

'And you like it?'

'Of course I like it! If you want, I could give you her number and she could do the same here.'

The thought of someone striding through the rooms, casting a baleful eye over the furnishings and then replacing the lot with expensive equivalents made her blood run cold. Or maybe she just had an economical streak.

'I'll do what I can,' she conceded, 'but don't blame me if you disagree with my tastes.' He inclined his head in a nod. 'And when it comes to choosing bigger things, then you'll have to find the time to pick them yourself.' Another nod. 'Good.'

'So that's settled?'

'For the moment.'

'Then why don't we leave here and do something altogether more productive…and enjoyable?'

His restlessness had evaporated. He felt invigorated. The house had been closing him in, closing them both in with its reminder of their reversed fortunes. What better solution than to go outside and leave its depressing presence behind? And what better way to voice the suggestion than in words of such blatant ambiguity that she could do nothing but flush at the latent connotations?

'What did you have in mind?' Laura asked warily.

'Well…the sun is shining. And I hanker to ride Barnabus again…I haven't ridden in months, not since I was in Argentina. Is he still as fiery as he once was?'

'You want to go *riding*?' Laura squeaked.

'Outrageous, I agree, but, yes, I do. For one thing, it's a waste to be inside when we can be outside and for another, I could use the opportunity to see the land and try and work out what needs doing.'

'Oh. Yes. Of course.' She glanced down at her clothes. 'I'll just go and get changed, shall I?'

A perfectly sensible suggestion, she told herself as she hurriedly shoved on a pair of jeans and an old sweatshirt. It was bright but breezy and very concealing. So why then did she feel just a little bit apprehensive? She couldn't keep the past totally locked away, could she?

He was waiting at the foot of the stairs for her, and he made damned sure that he gave her only a cursory glance.

'You're not really in the right gear,' Laura informed him, *en route* to the stables.

'I didn't think that I would end up on a horse or else I would have dressed differently.'

'You mean you have scruffy clothes?'

'Tut-tut. There you go. Pigeon-holing again.' But his voice was lazily amused. 'And for your information, I happen to have quite a lot of scruffy clothes hanging in my wardrobe.'

'Oh, really.' The sun, the ease of his conversation, the faint buzzing of the bees in the background, made her feel relaxed. 'Shabby jeans and faded tee shirts?'

'Absolutely. The shabbier and more faded, the better.'

She couldn't help it. She laughed, pushing open the stable door and expertly getting Barnabus ready before leading him out into the courtyard.

'Do you want me to come riding with you?' she asked, suddenly realising that she had expected to but that he might want to ride on his own. A lot of people preferred the peace of solitude rather than riding with someone else and having to make conversation.

'I would not go otherwise. Saddle up one of the others.'

'Old Lily won't be able to keep up with Barnabus,' Laura warned him, watching greedily as he stroked the horse, speaking to it in those low, soothing tones that sounded like waves lapping against the shore, getting it to trust him before he mounted.

She hurried off and was returning with her own horse just in time to see Gabriel mount Barnabus, his every move solid and confident and exquisitely graceful. Whatever gripes her father had had over Gabriel, he had never been able to deny that Gabriel was good with horses. Better than good. He seemed to belong on them.

Laura stood, riveted, as he settled onto Barnabus's back, the reins lightly held in one hand whilst he stroked the horse's mane with the other.

'Are you going to mount or are you going to stare at me for the rest of the day?'

His laconic question, when she hadn't been aware that he had been so much as looking in her direction, jerked her back to reality and she mounted her own horse with alacrity, pressing her knees firmly on either side to urge it forward.

'Ready?' He grinned with infuriating amusement. Her gut feeling was to launch into a lecture on the size of his ego, which had encouraged him to hallucinate that she had been watching him when in fact her thoughts had been a million miles away, but since it would have been patently untrue she contented herself with tugging the rein in her hand and nodding.

'Shall we skirt the boundary fence to the left and follow it round to that oak tree? The oak tree *is* still there, I take it?' He wondered if he could concentrate on anything as banal as fencing when this woman was riding alongside him. Lord, but she looked beautiful. The sun captured the fairness of her hair until it seemed to dazzle the eyes and her body looked alive on the back of her horse, every muscle firm and toned. Quintessentially the very opposite to every woman he had dated since he had loved and lost her.

Ah, but he hadn't lost her, had he? he reminded himself silkily. Because here she was, the wind blowing back her hair, her body slightly arched as she galloped at a steady speed alongside him. Sexy in the way only a totally natural woman could be sexy and soon to be his until such time as he no longer considered her a lost love, simply someone else he would have slept with along the way.

'The fencing is in a bit of a state,' Laura told him, pointing out the obvious as they both slowed to a trot to inspect it. She had worked up a sweat riding and now shoved up the sleeves of the jumper. 'Dad looked after it when we still had horses but over the years he only managed to keep up rudimentary repairs.' She turned to face him. 'I must have been a complete idiot not to have noticed what was going on.'

'We all make mistakes.'

Was it her imagination or did she detect something else behind that throwaway remark? Was he referring to her? A past mistake he had once made?

'Shall we continue?' she asked tightly, and he nodded as he shrewdly assessed the extensive repair work that would have to be undertaken.

They circled the huge area. There were entire tracts of fencing that had rotted over time. The money that should have been used to fix them redirected into betting and alcohol. When Gabriel thought about it, he could feel a murderous urge towards Peter Jackson, but aligned to that was a certain sympathy that he neither invited nor welcomed. The man must have been distraught to have let the whole lot go. The riding stables had been his life.

By the time they finally reached the oak tree he had seen enough to have a pretty good idea of the state of the rest.

He dismounted, tethered his horse, thereby ensuring that she did the same, and then sat down at the base of the tree, his legs drawn up, his arms resting loosely on his knees.

'Your trousers will be filthy when you get up,' Laura remarked, smugly aware that she was far more appropriately dressed.

'Sit down by me,' Gabriel commanded lazily. 'We need to talk about how we're going to approach the job of upgrading the land.' Which, he reckoned, should take about ten minutes. And after that...? He intended to stick to his plans for seduction and not be distracted by the buzzing inner voices that kept holding him back. He looked at her from under his lashes as she slowly walked towards him. He noted the unconscious elegance of her gait, the way she held her body like a dancer, utterly indifferent to how other people regarded her.

'It's been impossible trying to do anything about it,' Laura said apologetically. 'Since Dad died, I seem to have spent all my time in a nightmare of trying to work out finances.' She sighed and Gabriel made an angry noise under his breath.

'God, didn't the man have any idea what this would do to you? Leaving you in a situation like that?'

'He never thought he would just...I guess he thought that he would have time to get things back on track and so I would be spared the worry.' She looked down at the fields sprawled in front of them. From a distance, it all looked perfect. It was only when you got closer that you could see the signs of decay. It was the same for the house and the stables. 'You don't have to tell me that it's a far cry from how things used to be around here seven years ago.'

'I was not about to tell you any such thing.' He got up, brushing himself down, only to reposition himself on the grass, lying on it with his hands folded behind his head and his long legs crossed at the ankles.

'Shouldn't we be heading back now?'

'Oh, I think I'll enjoy this sun for a bit longer. Of course, you are free to head back whenever you want.' It was a gamble, but he didn't want her in any way to feel that she had been manipulated. Nevertheless, his body seemed to twist into several thousand knots in the few seconds of silence during which she decided what to do. If she got up and rode back to the house, then he would be forced to stay, at least for a short while and, whilst the scenery was enchanting, its appeal would vanish like a puff of smoke if she weren't here to enhance it.

'Oh, I might as well wait for you,' Laura said eventually, and he wondered whether she could hear his profound sigh of relief. He turned on his side, propping himself up on one elbow so that he could look at her.

'Why don't you come out of the shade of that tree and enjoy the sunshine? It is not that often we get weather like this in spring.'

'I know,' Laura agreed, pushing herself up and strolling over in his direction. 'Last year it rained solidly for spring. If you think the fields are bad now, you should have seen them then. They looked like a jungle.' She sat down, still keeping her distance, he noticed idly. 'Old Tom McBride came and trimmed them back for next to no pay.'

Gabriel allowed his eyes to stray to the bottom half of

her body, encased in faded, tight jeans and topped with laced-up old leather walking shoes. She was still sitting up with her arms stretched out behind her to support her body. His eyes lingered for a few seconds on the definition of her stomach under the sweatshirt, then moved lazily up-wards to the swell of her breasts. Bra or no bra? he won-dered. Difficult to tell under that thick cloth. Her head was flung back, her eyes closed as she enjoyed the sun.

'What is your relationship with the estate agent?' Gabriel asked.

Laura's eyes flicked open and she turned to look at him. 'Any estate agent in particular?'

'The blond one who looked as though he perhaps had not started shaving yet.'

'I don't know any estate agents who fit that description.'

'Little liar,' Gabriel drawled. 'Was he your lover? Was that how you got the job working there?'

'I should come across there and smack you on the face for implying that,' Laura said.

'Well, why don't you?' he invited with a soft laugh that sent goose-pimples racing across her skin. 'You can hit me as hard as you like for being such an insufferable, insulting boor…and then I can take my revenge for being hit…'

'Oh, yes,' Laura said on a breathless little laugh. Her heart was racing and every shred of common sense was telling her that she was playing with fire. But the way he was looking at her, his black eyes roving lazily and ca-ressingly over her face, sent shivers of excitement through her that were shattering common sense.

'What would you do?' she taunted. 'I know you, Gabriel, however much you've changed over the years. You wouldn't dream of laying a finger on me…'

'Oh, I wouldn't dream of it, would I?' He pushed him-self up and moved closer to her, close enough to touch her if he wanted to but not so close that she would feel his presence as a threat. Every muscle in his body felt alive. He would take this woman and under all the reasons he had logically worked out for himself, under all his arguments about levelling scores and evening scales, he was burning with the sheer, overpowering craving to take her simply because he found her irresistible...

CHAPTER SEVEN

'GABRIEL, n-no...'

'But I haven't done anything.' His slow smile was so devastating that it made the breath catch in Laura's throat. He'd mesmerised her. He mesmerised her then and he mesmerised her now, even though she knew that the divide between them stretched like a yawning gulf. The impassioned young boy had developed into a cynical predator and his motives were at best based on animal lust and at worst...she shivered to think.

But, God, the way his eyes were lingering on her face made her feel as though she were standing close to an open fire and on the edge of a precipice.

'I—I'm not a complete idiot,' Laura stuttered weakly, hugging herself.

'I never implied that you were. What are you wearing under that baggy sweatshirt of yours?'

'Wh-what?'

He gave a low, sexy laugh and continued to look at her. One long, hot look of burning intensity that seemed to send the heat spreading from the tips of her toes to the top of her scalp.

'Are you wearing a bra? You never used to when you went riding. I remember you once told me that you dreamed of riding on a beach, naked, and that the closest you could ever get to that was to ride without a bra under your jumper. But then, in those days, there were always a lot more people around. Now...here we are, alone on this little hill...'

'This is not an appropriate conversation.' She made a desperate effort to get back to normality but she couldn't tear her eyes away from him and her heart was pounding so hard that her ribcage felt as though it might crack at any moment. 'We're not the same two people now that we were then. I work for you. Have you forgotten? And you told me that you would never have a relationship with an employee.'

'Oh, but I am not talking about having a relationship. I am talking about making love. And rules, at the end of the day, are made to be broken.' He wasn't about to let her imagine for a minute that any kind of relationship was in the offing. He had offered her one of those once and had been rejected. This time, he would be brutally honest and he would let her come to him in the full knowledge that what he wanted and *all* he wanted was her delectable body.

He trailed his finger along her spine and smiled. 'No bra. I thought so. Some things never change.'

'Stop it!' Laura spun around so that she was facing him. That light touch had felt like an invasion, and, horrifyingly, an invasion she craved. 'Is that how you live your life, Gabriel? A series of episodes with women in bed? How sad.'

'Why is it sad?' Her mouth was spitting insults, he thought with gratification, but her chocolate eyes were telling another story, and he continued to devastate her with his look. 'Because you think that sex has to be accompanied by emotions? And since you never married, are you telling me that you have not slept with another man since me?'

'Of course I have,' Laura retorted scornfully, and his body stilled. He really hadn't expected her to say otherwise, but for reasons he could scarcely identify the thought of her lying in the arms of another man brought a surge of jealous bile rising to his throat.

'The effeminate little man at the estate agency?'

Trust Gabriel Greppi to be contemptuous of someone like Hugo, she thought with sudden anger. Just because Hugo was not built along the macho lines that he was and did not have the overpowering self-assurance that made him see the world and its female inhabitants as his own personal playground.

Oh, how he would love to think that she had spent seven years in a deep freeze, pining.

The fact that it was mostly true, something she was only now beginning to realise, made her even angrier.

'No, not Hugo!' she snapped, thrusting her face towards him.

'Who, then? And if he was so meaningful, where is he now?' It took all his strength not to give in to basic instinct and shake the answer out of her.

'His name was James Silcox, if you must know!' And what a mistake he had been. After four years of celibacy, she could see, in retrospect, that she had drifted into the relationship partly in a desperate attempt to alter the rut into which her love life had sunk and partly because her father had approved of him. It had been a disaster. His talent for being amusing had not concealed a clever mind, as she had optimistically imagined. He had been good-looking, witty and as empty as a shell. The relationship had lasted all of six months and then dwindled into a sporadic friendship, which was all it should ever have been in the first place. It had not escaped her notice that since her financial problems had come to light, even that had disappeared. She was no longer a desirable connection.

'And I don't know where he is now,' she finished truthfully.

'What happened? Were you too forceful for the poor boy?'

'Me? Forceful?'

'You don't play feminine games,' Gabriel told her, reaching out to brush some hair away from her face. 'And men tend to like their women to play feminine games.'

'You mean, batting eyelashes and pretending to be help-less even when they have nerves of steel?'

'Something like that.' He hadn't anticipated quite so much conversation. Women, he had always found, or at least those he had dated in the past, had always followed his lead, and lengthy conversation had never been high on his agenda. But then hadn't he always known that this particular woman was unique? In fact, he had forgotten how much he enjoyed just talking to her. 'Also...' he let his eyes drift casually over her baggy sweatshirt and faded jeans '...they tend to be impressed by a more...feminine look.' He knew that one would get to her and he grinned broadly when her expression reflected the expected reac-tion of sulky affront.

'Oh, well, thank you very much for that, Gabriel. You've just put your finger on why I haven't managed to find Mr Right. My taste in clothes hasn't been up to par. And I suppose all these little episodes in your sad, sad love life have had exquisite dress sense?' Was he aware of the flirtatious thread running through this conversation? she wondered frantically. Instead of fuming over his un-disguised insults, she was blossoming! The teasing, lazy look in his black eyes gave his words a sexy, bantering intonation that had every nerve in her body singing.

'They have,' he agreed gravely.

'And what would that exquisite dress sense be com-prised of?' she asked, stung by the comparisons she knew he must be making in his head between herself and his past conquests.

'Oh, the usual. Tight little dresses with plunging necklines and high, high heels.' And not one of them could light a candle next to this woman sitting right here, he thought suddenly, with her concealing clothes and lack of make-up. The thought of those heavy breasts, unfettered beneath the loose-fitting sweatshirt, turned him on in a way that no tight dresses and revealing necklines ever could. He savoured the moment when he could push up the thick cotton and feast his eyes on her bountiful body.

Laura wanted to ask him if he was so enamoured of voluptuous women in figure-hugging clothes, why then did he want to sleep with *her*? But she was too afraid of his answer to ask the question. God, was she so pathetic that she preferred to ignore the truth staring her in the face? Which was that he simply wanted to revisit old pastures and prove to them both that he could still have her if he wanted, no strings attached?

'Well, in that case, why don't you mount Barnabus and ride back to the house so that you can get away quickly and find yourself a suitably well-dressed woman?'

'Actually,' Gabriel drawled, his skin positively crawling with pleasure at this show of pique, 'there's something that is even sexier than tight-fitting clothes on a woman…'

'And what's that? Not that I'm interested.'

'*No* clothes on a woman.' The words dropped into the charged pool of electricity between them and he watched as the ripples began to fan out. 'No clothes on a woman, out in the open, surrounded by fields and trees.' The games were done and, whether she knew it or not, she wasn't going to slip away from him. 'The smell of warm sun on a naked body and the feel of grass under bare skin.'

A fine film of perspiration broke out over her body as

her imagination took wild flight. Her head was screaming at her to run away as fast as she could, but she couldn't move. She could just watch him close the small distance between them, and her eyes drooped as his mouth covered hers.

His hunger drove her backwards until she was lying on the grass, his body half over her as he pushed his tongue against hers and explored the warmth of her mouth with an urgency that was matched by her own. Her hands pressed against the side of his face and she arched back in sheer pleasure as he began kissing her neck and behind her ear.

'Do you want this, *querida*?' he murmured hoarsely. 'Because if you don't, then you had better tell me now. Before we both reach the point of no return.'

'Yes,' Laura whispered raggedly. 'No. Oh, I don't know, Gabriel.'

He stopped and looked down at her until her eyes flickered open. 'Tell me,' he commanded roughly, running one thumb along her eyebrow, and she turned her face into his hand and kissed his palm.

'Yes,' she admitted unsteadily. 'I want you, I want *this*.' And she knew exactly what *this* was, the act of making love, nothing more, nothing less.

'And I want to hear you say it,' Gabriel told her huskily. 'I want to hear you moan with delight. God, I want to feel you tremble under my arms, Laura.' Balancing on his elbow, he began to unbutton his shirt with his other hand, his fingers trembling until the shirt was finally hanging open and Laura curved her arms beneath it, delighting in the feel of his naked torso. She had watched him and imagined, but actually feeling him was beyond imagination, as was the dizzying sensation of coming back to a place where she belonged.

She eased his shirt off his shoulders, savouring each glimpse of hard, bronzed skin, and watched as he shrugged if off.

'Not exactly fair,' he murmured with a wicked gleam in his eye that had her blushing like a virgin bride instead of a woman who had lain countless times in this man's arms before.

'What's not fair?' she responded with a wicked, teasing smile of her own. She reached up to lick his mouth with the tip of her tongue and smiled as a low moan escaped him.

'My performing a striptease while you remain covered up like a Victorian damsel.'

He moved into a kneeling position, his legs straddling either side of her and watched, fascinated, as she drew the sweatshirt slowly upwards, exposing the firm paleness of her flat stomach, then those breasts, which he had been lusting after ever since he had first laid eyes on her again. A hot burst of desire exploded inside him, shocking him with its intensity. His hands itched to touch, but he restrained himself, savouring the prospect of possession. Instead, he continued looking at her, breathing unsteadily whilst she lay passively and bewitchingly beneath him.

'Having fun?' he smiled crookedly and she stretched languidly in response, raising her hands over her head. She wanted to faint from the intense pleasure of just having those eyes roam over her semi-nude body.

'Are you?' she replied. Stupid question. Whatever he felt for her, whatever dubious reasons he had for making love with her, there was no doubt in her head that he still wanted her and, Lord, how she still wanted him. Sheer physical need was now in the driver's seat.

'Never had so much fun in my life before.' Their eyes

met and she gave him a smile that was enchantingly, teasingly feminine.

She reached down to cup her breasts with her hands, inviting him to do more than just watch, and Gabriel sank towards her offering with a groan of submission, burying his face against her soft mounds and nuzzling them with his mouth and tongue until Laura was whimpering with pleasure.

The ragged sound that was wrenched from her lips as his mouth closed over one tautened nipple was the sound of absolute abandonment.

Gabriel dimly heard it and felt like a young adolescent on the brink of orgasm just from the touch of his fantasy woman. In the distant past, when they had stolen their love-making sessions in the office, their passion had been muted by the unspoken thought that they might, just might, be interrupted. Now, with miles of deserted fields around them, they could be as vocal as they wanted and her cries of pleasure were like music to his ears.

But he wasn't going to rush a minute of this.

He took his time, devoting his undivided attention to her beautiful breasts and loving the feel of her writhing beneath him and begging him not to stop. As if he were even capable of stopping!

He licked her breasts and then trailed his tongue along her stomach, which tasted warm. And her smell was the smell of pure woman, without any of those lingering traces of perfume that did nothing for him.

He undid the top button of her jeans, then the zip, and gently eased them down her long legs until he could easily pull them off and toss them to one side.

'That's not fair,' Laura said huskily, repeating his teasing observation of earlier on, and he grinned at her.

'So it isn't,' he drawled, catching her eyes and holding

them, although not for long. The need to look at that beautiful, bronzed body was far too tempting just to make do with his eyes.

She watched with greedy yearning as he shrugged off his already unbuttoned shirt, then deliberately took his time with his trousers. With unconscious provocation, Laura's fingers strayed to the top of her underwear and she casually slipped them under to caress the fair, soft curls as she continued to drink him in with her eyes.

God, the woman couldn't possibly know what she was doing to him, Gabriel thought with another savage thrust of undiluted desire. He watched the idle movement of her hand under the flimsy cotton of her underwear and any thoughts of taking his time disappeared under the need to touch her again.

His trousers were kicked aside, quickly followed by his silk boxer shorts until he was standing in front of her feverish gaze in all his proud, masculine and very impressive nudity.

A slow, satisfied and eminently cat-like smile curved her wide mouth.

Wasn't it supposed to be the other way around? Gabriel thought wryly. Wasn't *he* supposed to be the cat in command of its very luscious prey?

'Touching yourself, *cara*?' he enquired lazily as he sank down to join her on the warm grass and he covered her hand with his own.

'Of course I'm not!' Laura protested. She stroked the side of his face and felt a lump gather at the back of her throat. All this would become was another memory to add to the collection, she thought sadly. She meant nothing to him and he had made that perfectly clear.

He took her hand and kissed the tip of each of her fin-

gers with such infinite tenderness that she could almost kid
herself that there was some emotion there.

There was nothing to be gained from dwelling on it, she
thought, pulling him fiercely towards her and kissing him,
liking it better when he yanked off her last remaining item
of clothing.

'Want to play rough, do you, little tiger?' He laughed
softly into her mouth.

'It's been a long time.'

'Feel free to make as much noise as you want,' he returned, moving directly over her so that his hardness
brushed against her belly and set up a series of sweet sen-
sations inside her. He hooked his arms under her back so
that she curved up towards him and began to ravage her
breasts.

Then, without any thought of teasing her further, he
moved down to part her thighs with his hand and began
plundering between her legs. He felt it when she curled
her fingers into his hair and then she began obeying his
strict instructions that she should make as much noise as
she wanted.

At some point, lost in the daze of tasting her, he felt her
tug his head up to tell him that he had to stop, that he was
driving her crazy, and then it was *his* turn to be ravaged
by *her*.

It was something he had not experienced for a very long
time. The women he had dated in the past had preferred
him to make all the moves and that had always suited him
perfectly, unconsciously maintaining the control that had
become part and parcel of his dominant personality.

Now *she* was taking control and he found himself enjoying every minute of it as she straddled him and, after
taking her fill of every inch of his body, sank onto his

engorged manhood and began moving in a way that was unbelievably erotic.

Her breasts dangled tantalisingly by his face, brushing his mouth until he caught one in his hands and began suckling on the tight bud, whilst her body continued to move over him, grinding harder until they reached that point of no return and crossed it.

Laura finally lay down on him, spent and satiated, and he stroked her hair.

'So,' she said seriously, rolling off him to lie on the grass at his side, 'I guess it goes without saying that what we did was…a big mistake…' She sat up and reached for her clothes, only to find herself pulled back down as one big hand descended on her shoulder.

'What do you think you are doing?' They looked at one another, both on their sides, facing each other.

'We have to get back to the house, Gabriel. I was getting dressed. We…we shouldn't have done what…what we just did. You know that.'

'Why not?'

'Because sex is just going to complicate everything.'

'Oh, is it, now?' He idly began to stroke her breasts, enjoying the way her body was reacting to his feather touch. Forget what she was saying about sex complicating everything. She still wanted him. It was obvious in the way her nipples were hardening under his lingering finger and in the way her breathing was beginning to sound raspy.

For a while just then he had been so lost in the rapture of touching this woman, feeling her naked body, that he had almost forgotten the whole point of the exercise. This, he reminded himself, was the woman who had turned him away and it was only now, being with her again, wanting her the way he did, that Gabriel could see how affected his life had been by the rejection.

'Yes, it is,' Laura said, shifting to move, and he caught her wrist with his hand and, after kissing her palm, turned his eyes to hers.

'Why? Did you not enjoy what we just did?'

'You know I did.'

'Mmm. I know.' He smiled lazily and began stroking her thigh until she gave an involuntary gasp of pleasure as her body responded. He leant forward and kissed her delicately on her mouth until she lay back down so that he could lean over her and continue his exquisite exploration of her lips with his tongue.

And this time their love-making was slow and languorous. He touched every inch of her with such infinite gentleness that her body wanted to explode from sheer *want*. When she would have tugged him up from those most intimate caresses a woman could have, he captured her restless hand with his steady one and continued caressing her, devoting himself entirely to bringing her so close to the peak of orgasm that she was panting, only to replace his inquisitive tongue with little kisses.

By the time she lay spent by his side, the fragile spring warmth was beginning to recede and, by mutual consent, they both got dressed and began the ride back to the house.

'I'll help you muck them out,' he told her, the first words they had exchanged since their shatteringly prolonged love-making.

'Honestly, you don't have to. I…I'm perfectly capable of handling it on my own.'

'I realise I don't have to, but I want to.'

It was a relief that the physical demands of tending to the horses allowed Laura time to try and get her frantic thoughts into some kind of order. Not that she wasn't helplessly aware of Gabriel working right there alongside her. Somewhere along the line, he had removed his shirt and it seemed that wherever she looked her eyes crashed into his bare-backed torso with its hard, muscular strength and tightly packed muscle.

'Right,' she said weakly, after forty-five minutes of solid work conducted in silence, 'I think we can call it a day here.'

Gabriel stood back and looked at her. Her hair was damp with perspiration and she had shoved up the sleeves of her sweatshirt. With deliberate slowness, he put back on his shirt, leaving it unbuttoned.

'Feels like old times,' he drawled. 'I haven't mucked out for years.'

'I'm surprised you never bought any horses,' Laura said, grasping at this little straw of conversational normality. She dragged her eyes away from him and moved towards the stable door.

'I thought about it,' Gabriel replied, watching her as she carefully avoided his gaze. 'But horses need constant attention and upkeep and...' he shrugged '...my working hours are too unpredictable.' He walked behind her and closed the door behind him. He could read DISCOMFORT written all over her in huge capital letters, and perversely wanted to snatch her back to him.

He rested his hand loosely on her neck and felt her flinch. Dammit, she hadn't been uncomfortable back there out in the open! Oh, no, she had been abandoned and uninhibited and utterly in his possession!

'Relax,' he told her softly.

'Relax? How can you possibly expect me to relax?' Laura swung round to look at him, her eyes wide with confusion.

'Easily,' Gabriel said smoothly. 'We have just had mind-blowing sex. You should be feeling very relaxed.'

'I should be heading for the nearest river to jump in,' Laura said bitterly. 'We should never have made love. It was a mistake and it won't happen again!'

'We will discuss this inside. When we have both had a shower and something to eat.'

'There's nothing to discuss,' Laura muttered, turning away, hugging herself tightly.

For the moment, Gabriel thought, he would leave her nursing her thoughts of regret and actually thinking that their love-making might really be a one-off episode.

'And shouldn't you be heading back to London?' she flung at him.

'In due course. But definitely not in this state.' He looked down at himself, covered in bits of straw, and Laura reluctantly admitted that he had a point. Not to mention the small fact that the house belonged to him anyway, so he could have however many damned showers he wanted!

'I'll get you a towel,' she said as soon as they were in the front door.

'And get one for yourself whilst you are about it.' He looked at her without smiling, but the intent was stamped all over his face.

'What are you talking about?' A frisson of excitement and alarm ripped through her.

'As we are both in dire need of a shower, then I suggest we do it together.' And when she opened her mouth to protest, he covered it swiftly with his own and felt her body melt. Oh, yes. Did she really think that she could run away from him now? Did she really imagine that he would allow her to do that?

'Didn't you hear a word...th-that I just said, Gabriel?'

'Heard and absorbed every word, *amante*. Which is not to say that I agree with a single one of them.' To emphasise his point, he slipped his hands under her jumper and placed his hands under the crease of her breasts. 'What we did was not a mistake. We wanted one another and we still want one another, and there is no point in your pretending otherwise.' He could feel the rapid beating of her heart under her ribcage.

'We can't bring the past back.' Laura heard the unsteady tremor of her voice with dismay. She should be thrusting him away, flying up those stairs as fast as her legs could carry her, but she couldn't move a muscle.

'Nor can we forget it,' he replied fiercely. 'Why don't you tell me that it was all a mistake...now...?' His hands covered her breasts and he began rousing her with masterful precision, touching her nipples and setting them aflame with longing. They half walked, half stumbled, still united, until he was pressing her back against the wall, and with her in that position he moved one hand to her thigh and began rubbing her there, there where she could do nothing but respond, his fingers firm as they pushed against the crease of the denim until she was half crying out.

She surrendered. He felt it the instant her arms wrapped around him and she blindly searched for his mouth.

'Now, what about that shower?' he broke away to murmur and she looked at him with a dazed expression, then smiled.

His tactics, he admitted minutes later as the warm water shot jets down at them both in the shower cubicle, left a lot to be desired, but all was fair in love and war.

Strangely, though, he didn't just want her to yield to him because she couldn't resist the tug of what they did to one another in the sack.

'Your hair needs washing,' he said, swivelling her away

from him and reaching for the bottle of shampoo so that he could trickle some into her wet hair and begin massaging. 'And this is not the way to do it,' he murmured huskily, when she gave a sensuous little whimper of pleasure and curved her back against him so that he had no choice, as a red-blooded male, but to wrap his arms around her and bury his mouth against her neck.

'You're right.' She squirmed until she was facing him, slippery with soap and water, and their quick shower, as it turned out, took them a lot longer than they had anticipated.

This was what he wanted. Or so he told himself in the warmth of the kitchen, holding a glass of chilled wine in his hand and looking at her as she busied herself in the kitchen, having insisted that he sit down and let her cook.

At his beck and call. One touch, and she was on fire. Click his fingers and she would melt in his arms.

So why was there still a thread of dissatisfaction gnawing away at the pit of his stomach? Had he not achieved exactly what he had wanted? If he turned his back now and walked away, he knew that she would be the one to hurt, so why the ache? He owned the house, the land, her body. He had got his revenge and now he felt sullied, somehow, by it.

'There was no need to put yourself to all this trouble,' he said abruptly, and she turned to face him with a frown.

'What's the matter? What's wrong?'

'Nothing is wrong. Why should anything be wrong?' he asked irritably.

'No reason whatsoever,' Laura replied, covering the frying-pan with a lid and drying her hands on a towel. She reached for her wineglass on the counter and took a sip of wine, then she perched against the ledge of the counter and folded her arms. 'You're free to go any time you want,

Gabriel,' she said coolly. 'Don't imagine that because we've slept together that there's any need for you to try and play the gentleman now. In case you'd conveniently forgotten, *you* were the one who suggested staying on for something to eat.'

'And in case *you'd* conveniently forgotten, *you* were only too delighted at the suggestion.' Flushed, as she had been, after their third bout of love-making! For some reason, the thought of her murmuring things she thought he wanted to hear when in the throes of passion made his teeth snap together in fury.

It was something of which Laura did not want to be reminded. Let that be a lesson to her, she thought angrily. Nothing between them was normal and it was pointless pretending that it could ever be! They were not some domesticated little couple playing at happy families. They had made love but love was the last thing that came into the act. The thought of him sitting there, squirming because he would rather be off now that he had slept with her, filled her with mortification.

'It seemed sensible!' she shot back. 'Not that I have much choice, anyway! After all, this *is* your house. I am only acting the part of dutiful employee.'

'And was that what you were doing earlier on?' he rasped. 'Acting the part of the dutiful employee?'

Laura was the first to look away. She didn't want to see the jeering cynicism stamped in those beautiful black eyes. More importantly, she didn't want him to see the furious, blinding panic in her *own* eyes.

God, she thought with dawning, incredulous horror, I've fallen in love with him. All over again. Maybe, she thought with clammy dismay, she had never fallen *out* of love with him. She had just managed to submerge it all until he came back into her life and then, well, it had just been a question of time before she'd catapulted back into his arms. She could have coped better if she had thought that she had been acting the part of the dutiful employee!

'No,' she whispered numbly.

She had turned away and Gabriel, his body tense, wanted desperately for her to turn back to him so that he could read what was going on in that seductive head of hers. He took a few deep breaths to calm himself and to regain some of his self-control.

'Look,' he said to her back, 'there is no point in us arguing with one another.' Why the hell wouldn't she look at him? The thought that he might have blown it filled him with sudden, suffocating dread. 'I just did not want you to feel that you had to slave over a kitchen stove to cook food for me when I would more than happily have taken you somewhere to eat.'

'I had to cook for myself anyway,' Laura muttered, which shoved his simmering anger a few notches higher. She had succumbed to lust and so, heck, why not invite him to eat with her? Not as if she were putting herself out!

'Women, home-cooked meals and me do not mix.' Pride slammed into place with ferocious ease. 'It's been my experience,' he said dismissively, 'that a woman who cooks food wants more than I am ever prepared to give.'

'In which case,' Laura replied with equal dismissiveness, 'you have nothing to fear from me in that area.'

'Because all you want is sex?'

Because it's all I can get and that's better than nothing. 'Why not?' She shrugged and began putting plates and cutlery on the table. Brave words but she couldn't meet his eyes. She couldn't bear to see the relief in his eyes that she wasn't going to clutter his high-powered life with unwanted complications. 'We're both adults,' she said with a tight smile. 'Isn't it good that we understand each other?'

CHAPTER EIGHT

GABRIEL frowned at the computer screen in front of him. He could vaguely register the detailed report staring back at him and the numbers indicating that a takeover made six months previously was beginning to show the profit he had predicted, but his eyes were glazed.

When the phone rang, he leapt at the receiver and grabbed the opportunity to shove his chair back at an angle that offered him a view through the opened door into the sitting room where Laura was busily discussing colours and paints with three men.

He had decided, he had told her, that he needed to be on hand to supervise the beginnings of work being done on the house. This wasn't a company takeover, he had told her grandly, he was personally involved with this particular purchase, he had to be there for her to consult freely whenever she felt she needed to. When she had drily reminded him of the need to trust his workforce, namely her, he had swept aside the objection with a careless wave of his hand and words to the effect that it would be easier for him to work from the house as opposed to having her travel down every single time she needed to make a decision about something. That was the whole point of communications these days, he had explained, stilling the protest she had been about to utter. E-mail facilities, fax machines, computers allowed total mobility.

Within twenty-four hours he had moved in lock, stock and barrel, propelled by an urgent need that he himself did not fully comprehend. He just knew that he had to be around her.

Now, he stretched out his long legs on the dining table, which was big enough to implement as his desk, and looked, with satisfaction, at the tall, lithe blonde who was obviously having absolutely no trouble whatsoever in dealing with three of the men she had employed. She needed his presence here like a fish needed a tree, he thought to himself as he went through the motions of dealing with his secretary on the other end of the phone. But she needed his body. Of that there was no question. When the day was done, she would slide into bed with him, warm and willing and insatiable in her demands. It should have been enough. In fact, he knew that he should be tiring of her, getting ready to deliver his final trump card, namely his withdrawal, and thereby complete the business he had set into motion.

When he replaced the receiver, he remained sitting as he was, his fingers linked loosely on his lap, and pondered the niggling question of why her physical acquiescence was proving to be more of a frustration than if she had denied him her body totally.

Because, he reflected, he wanted her mind as well. Did she give tuppence for him at all? Was there anything there for her apart from the great sex? When she chatted to him and laughed at some of the things he said, was it done out of some obscure sense of obligation or duty or, worse, guilt because sex should be accompanied by at least some measure of amicability? Lord, the questions nagged away at him until he finally stood up in utter frustration and strode into the sitting room.

'What's going on in here?' he asked with a strained smile. 'Anything that I should be aware about?' Just being within a few feet of her made his fingers itch and he shoved his hands firmly into his pockets whilst he continued to survey the room, now stripped of its wallpaper, in the manner of someone who knew what they were looking at.

'I'm sorry.' Laura smiled. 'Did we disturb you? It must be a little disruptive trying to work in the room opposite. Why don't you close the door to the dining room?'

'I did not come here to isolate myself away from what is happening,' he muttered irritably, his dark eyes sliding across to dwell on the bewitching picture she presented, all ruffled hair and overalls that should have diminished her appeal but instead heightened it. 'After all, it *is* my house.' Had he just said that? A sullen, infantile observation that had her narrowing her eyes fractionally? 'What are these colours on the walls?' he asked, pointing at the streaks, and he allowed himself to be carried along with the flow as she began discussing what should be used where, whilst the plasterer made him run his hands along the walls, which would need resurfacing, and the electrician pointed to various sockets and made intelligent sounding remarks about the wiring in the house.

Out of the corner of his eye, Gabriel watched her face become animated as she discussed what could be done and tried to prise time scales out of the three men.

He could hear the sound of yet more men working on the floor above, pulling up the worn carpets and stripping the walls of yet more wallpaper.

On the spur of the moment he made a decision.

'I think we can leave the workforce here to get on with the basics,' he announced, pulling her to one side.

'Leave them and do what? My job is to be here, supervising.'

'I am temporarily altering your duties,' Gabriel informed her. He captured her arm with his hand and ex-

plained to the three men that they would be on their own
for a few hours and could they manage. 'You know where
everything is,' he continued, still grasping her hand just in
case she attempted to wriggle free to play the damned dil-
igent employee. 'Tea, coffee, milk. Help yourself in our
absence and we will see you later.'

This, Laura fulminated as she hurriedly changed in the
bathroom into some clean, fairly respectable clothes, was
the problem. All was fine when they were making love.
Everything could be forgotten then in the midst of explo-
sive passion, but the minute they were in a normal situation
he just couldn't help reminding her who was boss. She
worked for him and he never spared a thought for how she
felt. Why should he? she asked herself repressively. She
was his employee by day and his sex slave by night until
he tired of one or both duties and dismissed her. Emotion
did not enter into it and feelings were never, ever discussed.

The minute she stormed down the stairs, Gabriel could
see that her simmering anger at his high-handed attitude
was heading for boiling point, and he countered it with a
conciliatory smile.

'My apologies for behaving with such despicable arrogance,' he told her before she could let rip. 'Forgive me?'
His dark eyes appreciatively took in the vanilla cord trousers and the blue and cream checked shirt that she had
slung casually over a figure-hugging cropped blue vest.

'I told you it was a bad idea moving in here. You don't
need to keep a constant watch on me. I'm not going to do
anything outrageous with your precious décor!'

'You look enchanting.'

'I beg your pardon?'

'Enchanting and utterly, utterly irresistible.' He smiled
very slowly and watched as the storm in her eyes gave

way to pink-cheeked silence. 'Would you be horribly offended if I told you that I had to come in there and take you somewhere private so that I could thoroughly seduce you?'

'I would tell you that completing this job would take for ever if you didn't learn to control your...'

'My...?' Gabriel prompted silkily.

'Your carnal urges.' Just saying it, though, made her feel like jelly inside. And the beast knew it! 'Where are we going anyway? I really feel as though I ought to be supervising these men just to make sure that nothing goes horribly wrong.'

'They are stripping walls, pulling up carpets and doing the odd bit of plastering,' Gabriel said wryly, slipping his arm around her waist and leading her outside to the car. 'There is a limit as to how confused they can get by those very simple tasks.' Before he unlocked the car, he swung her around to face him. He couldn't help himself. It felt like years since he had touched her, even though it was only a matter of a few hours.

'Have you ever been ravished in a car?' he murmured, threading his fingers through her hair and tilting her face up to his.

'You still haven't told me where we're going,' Laura said unsteadily. A few well-chosen words and she was putty in his hands! It was pathetic. Or maybe it was just love and love had no qualms about turning a sane human being into an unthinking idiot.

'So I haven't.' He released her, unlocked the car and then opened the door for her, leaning down once she had tucked her long legs inside. 'But you'll be pleased to hear that I have not stolen you away simply to satisfy my needs.' Yes, he thought sourly, he could turn her on all right, just as he always had been able to years ago.

Her velvety brown eyes looked at him in bewilderment. 'You mean we're actually going somewhere?'

'Call it a drive to have a look at some interior design. And there will be no need for us to rush, because whilst you were changing I told Pete Clarke to make sure that the house is locked and everyone out when he leaves this evening. I thought it better, really, because it is a bit of a drive and who knows, *cara*, we might want to stop *en route*?'

'Certainly nowhere that involves pulling up down a narrow side lane,' Laura admonished as soon as he was in the car and pulling out of the drive, but just thinking about it was enough to bring a smile to her lips. 'I'm way too old for that kind of thing and, besides, we're both far too tall for making love in the cramped back seat of your car. Even if it *is* a very big car.'

'You might be tall but you're as supple as a piece of elastic,' Gabriel replied, his eyes fixed on the road. He gave a wicked grin that set her pulses racing. 'But maybe you're right,' he conceded ruefully.

'So tell me where we're going, Gabriel.'

'We are going to my place in Berkshire. I want you to have a look at my house and tell me what you think, about the style of the décor.'

'You mean get an idea of what you like?'

He shrugged. 'Actually, I hired a team of people to do the house for me. Lack of time.' Or inclination, for that matter.

'And do you like what they've done?' Laura felt a burning curiosity to see this man whom she adored in his surroundings.

'It is very grand.'

'You don't sound awfully certain, Gabriel.'

'I thought I liked it, but now I'm not too sure.' Quite

an admission and one that took him by surprise. He had never had any complaints about his mansion before but now, having seen her at work with her colour charts and wallpaper books, he had been overtaken by the feeling that his mansion, kitted out in the most lavishly expensive style by the most sought-after professional interior designers, was not suited to his tastes after all.

'If you don't like the way it's been decorated, then what's the point of taking me there?' Laura asked, and he began irritably drumming the steering wheel with his thumb.

'I thought you might enjoy getting away from the riding stables for a day,' Gabriel said and he immediately wondered whether she was as conscious of the petulance in his voice as he was. 'I mean, when was the last time you got away, Laura?'

'Got away from the house?'

'House, county, country, whatever!'

'There's no need to start shouting.'

'*I am not shouting!*' A simple plan, he thought, to close the books and put the past behind him, and look at where he was now! The woman had managed to get under his skin in ways he could never have imagined! From being a man permanently in control, he had become someone who swung from mood to mood with alarming irregularity, not that she even noticed, never mind cared!

'Oh, good.' She glanced wryly at him and their eyes met in a split second of perfect accord which, ludicrously, made him want to stop the car and give her a hug. A hug, he thought with exasperation! Since when did *hugs* feature in his grand plans of seduction and revenge.

'Well…' Laura chewed her lip and thought. 'I *have* been to London within the last year…'

'Have you? Who with?' He was in there before his brain

could tell his mouth to keep silent, but when he glanced sideways at her she hardly seemed to have registered his querulous demand.

'As for leaving the country…no, I can't remember the last time I actually left the country to go on holiday any-where.' Laura sighed. When she had been growing up and living in the lap of luxury, trips abroad had been regular annual events. Both her parents had been disinclined to leave the riding stables for too long in the care of someone else, but even so they had always had two weeks in the sun somewhere over winter and a week during the Easter holidays. 'Why? Are you offering?' she teased, and when he remained silent she realised that she had crossed an invisible boundary. And one she should have seen from a mile off, she thought miserably. Holidays would have con-stituted something more than just sex and there was no way that he would have considered that option.

'What if I did?' Gabriel asked with mild curiosity. The thought of going on a holiday with the woman sitting next to him was like a promise of paradise and he had to grimly remind himself that he had felt just like this seven years ago when the prospect of marriage had beckoned.

Laura, looking at the stern profile, could almost read what was going on in his head. The thought of going any-where with her that might indicate a normal relationship was abhorrent to him. It was written in block letters on his unsmiling face. Did he imagine that she would jump at the chance for an all-expenses-paid vacation now that she was indebted to him?

'I would refuse, of course,' she said lightly, turning away and staring with unseeing eyes at the fast-moving countryside around them. 'A dutiful employee never aban-dons her job when it's only just started.'

Her glibly spoken answer hit him like a hammer in his gut but he forced himself to nod curtly in agreement.

'How much further do we have to go?' Laura asked as his taut silence thickened around them. In the blink of an eye the light-hearted banter between them had evaporated and she knew, once again, how fragile it really was, how easily it was obliterated by one wrong word or one dangerous sentence. 'Tell me about your house. How long have you been living there?'

Gabriel expelled his breath and shook his head slightly. 'What can I say about my house? I bought it five years ago when the property market had slumped. I thought it would prove to be a worthwhile financial investment, and I was right. It has…eight bedrooms and I lose count of the reception rooms. A lot.'

'And you entertain quite a bit? I can't imagine you entertaining. You would frighten all your guests.' She saw his shoulders relax and a small smile replace the hard expression on his face. Ridiculously, she felt a spurt of pleasure that she could manage to shift his mood. He surely couldn't be that emotionally cold towards her if he could respond to her in that way, could he? Could he?

'Should I take that as a compliment?' he asked, flicking her a glance.

'Depends. Do you want to be thought of as scary?'

'Sometimes it helps in business,' Gabriel told her truthfully. 'Especially when you are an outsider. No matter that I have lived here for years. I am an Argentinian and you, of all people, should know how strong the old-school tie can be.' But there was no bitterness or resentment in his voice when he said this.

'I can't imagine that anyone would let old-school ties stop them from dealing with you, Gabriel, and you know it. You're way too charismatic to be ignored.'

'Now *that* I do take as a compliment. Although...' he lingered musingly before continuing '...you seem to be doing a rather good job of ignoring me at the moment.'

'Really. And what should I be doing?'

'My thigh feels a little stiff at the moment.' This was better. He was discovering that when it came to the physical, he was supremely in control, but whenever the emotional started creeping in, which it seemed to do a little too often for his liking, then his control disappeared like a puff of smoke. 'Must be all the driving,' he said helpfully. 'Perhaps you could massage it just a little...?'

'Isn't that a little dangerous when you're at the steering wheel?' Laura asked innocently and Gabriel grinned, back in the driver's seat in more ways than one.

'Perhaps you're right.' Just as well that there was a convenient turning less than five minutes later, and, because they had avoided the motorway, it was simplicity itself to go down sufficient winding turns to leave all signs of traffic behind.

'I know what you said about being too old and too tall,' Gabriel drawled, killing the engine and relaxing back against his car door so that he could look at her with lazy thoroughness, 'but I couldn't resist the temptation to discover whether you were right...'

A little over an hour later, Laura found out that she was neither...and nor was he.

When, she thought to herself as they approached the roundabouts and traffic lights that were the hallmark of suburbia, would she be able to look at this man and resist him? When would she be able to hear his voice, redolent with its soft, sexy come-on, and not feel every bone in her body melt?

More disturbingly, what was going to happen to her when he got sick of revisiting old territory and vanished, leaving her behind to pick up the pieces and start again? It seemed that they were living in a vacuum, where sex was the integral force, but whilst she was spinning away into the fantasy realms of love, he was merely enjoying her for a short while, enjoying the thought of controlling the woman who had turned him down. He wasn't spinning away anywhere.

She was barely aware of the change in the scenery. From passing estates to more open land where houses lay unglimpsed down avenues leading away from the main road.

His car turned down one of these imposing avenues and Laura blinked with a start to the view of a sprawling, ranch-style mansion, which loomed imposingly ahead of them.

'Your house?' She gaped incredulously and Gabriel half smiled.

'My house,' he agreed, slowing the car to park to one side of the drive. 'Like it?'

'It's very...impressive,' Laura said with resounding understatement. 'Very...big. Well, huge, really.'

She had to stand and stare once she was out of the car, whilst he patiently waited, watching her through narrowed eyes.

'It seems a bit magnificent for one person,' Laura finally volunteered, following him towards the imposing front door.

'Like I said, I originally bought it as a financial investment and as such it has been worth every penny.'

'There's more to life than money.'

'Really? I have yet to encounter it.' He opened the front door and stood aside to let her through.

Breathtaking enough on the outside, it was a designer's paradise on the inside. Wooden floors gleamed and seemed to stretch endlessly and matched perfectly with the heavy cream of the wallpaper, and through open doors she could glimpse a harmony of rich colours and thick curtains that hung to the ground in swirls.

The house had been cunningly designed on various levels, so from where she stood, with her back to the front door, Laura could see the staircase curve towards the left, where a luxurious sitting area overlooked the main entrance and presumably led to one wing of the house, before winding up towards the right wing of the house.

'If this is the sort of thing you like,' she joked nervously, 'then you're going to hate Oakridge House when it's finished. Lord, Gabriel, I almost feel as if I should remove my shoes just in case the shiny polished wood gets scuffed.' It was meant as a light-hearted observation but she could see from the thinning of his mouth that he hadn't cared for it.

'Don't be ridiculous, Laura. Come on, I will show you to the kitchen and we can have something to drink before we have a look around.' This was a mistake, he thought grimly. She hated this place and he was disgusted to find that he was now seeing it through her eyes as well and not much liking what he saw.

They bypassed rooms, into which Laura sneaked quick, fascinated peeks until they came to the kitchen, which, much as she might have expected, was everything anyone could want from a kitchen. Wood, chrome and cream gleamed with showroom brightness.

'Lovely,' she said faintly, and he glowered at her.

'You hate it. Why not be honest and admit it? I won't get annoyed.' He was so annoyed, in fact, that it felt good to add, with deliberate casualness, 'What you think does not affect me at all.'

'I don't hate it,' Laura said stubbornly, folding her arms. Did he have to spell out his position with such relentless indifference? 'And I would love a cup of coffee,' she continued, 'if you can locate it. These counters seem very clear of anything useful. I mean—' she could feel her hurt gathering some much-needed momentum '—what the heck is that?' She pointed at a silver gadget on the counter by the stove, which was so dazzlingly bright that you very nearly needed sunglasses to look at it.

'It's a…ah…juice extractor.'

'And that?'

'Cappuccino maker.'

'Which you're going to use to make my cup of coffee?'

'I prefer the ordinary kettle.' He had ruffled her beautiful feathers with his dismissive put-down, and Gabriel felt a twinge of disproportionate delight.

'Then why on earth did you waste your good money on a cappuccino maker? Huh? If you preferred *the ordinary kettle*? More money than sense.'

'I did not *buy* it, as a matter of fact.'

'Oh, I see. It just landed on your counter one morning from outer space.'

Gabriel threw back his head and laughed. 'It *does* look a little terrifyingly alien,' he agreed.

'And do you know how to use it?'

'I…'

'You don't know!' Laura crowed, grinning. 'What did I just say about more money than sense? I bet you're scared to go anywhere near it in case it explodes if you press the wrong button!'

'You are utterly incorrigible, woman.'

'And utterly right as well. So what other gadgets do you have concealed in this high-tech kitchen which you're too scared to use?'

Gabriel couldn't help it. He grinned sheepishly back at her and shrugged. 'The microwave can be a little uncooperative sometimes,' he admitted ruefully, wondering how on earth he had ever managed to feel remotely comfortable in a kitchen where most of the appliances seemed designed to repel casual use.

'So how on earth do you manage to fend for yourself?' Laura asked, folding her arms and subjecting him to a penetrating, quizzical stare.

The urge to tell her that what he needed was a good woman to fend for him was so strong that it left him shaken.

'I have staff,' he muttered, and she nodded with superior condescension.

'Handy.'

'It is one of the privileges money buys.' Gabriel wondered how she would look in an apron, cooking for him, tending to his every need. Try as he did to turn the image into a purely sexual one, all he could picture was the leggy blonde in front of him sitting at a kitchen table, a beaten old pine kitchen table, listening to him talk about his day, soothing away his stress.

Good God!

'Maybe we should leave the coffee for later,' he muttered, turning away so that she couldn't see any tell-tale darkening of his cheeks. 'I might as well show you around the rest of the house and, please...' he slid his eyes over to where she was standing, looking at him with her head inclined '...feel free to speak your mind.'

'Okay,' Laura replied airily. 'I will.'

Twenty minutes later and Gabriel was beginning to regret his open invitation. She had voiced her opinions on everything, from the colour of the walls to the choice of paintings hanging on them, from the design of the furniture to its level of comfort. In the sitting area she had bounced experimentally on the long pale blue sofa and pronounced it too firm.

'It may look attractive,' she had told him, sweeping imperious eyes over the sofa and chairs, which, from his vague recollections, had cost a small fortune, 'but sofas should be squashy. If you would prefer something along these lines, then you'd better tell me now, so that I know what to order or, rather, which stores to send you to for you to decide.'

'I cannot possibly make a decision like that on my own. I wouldn't know where to begin.'

'Now I'm supposed to see you as the Helpless Male?' Laura had shot him a disbelieving, sceptical look. 'You still haven't answered my question. Firm or squashy?'

'Squashy.'

'Patterned or plain?'

'What...' he had almost fallen into the trap of telling her to choose anything *she* liked, but had caught himself in the nick of time '...would you suggest? You are the designer.'

'Something warm and patterned,' Laura had said. 'Something with ethnic overtones, maybe in terracottas and greens.'

'Fine.'

And every room had been subjected to the same critical eye. By the time they were heading up the stairs to the bedroom wing of the house, Gabriel was fast developing a keen sense of loathing for most of his furnishings.

After guest room number two, Laura stood in front of him, frowning, her hands on her hips.

'I'm getting very mixed messages here, Gabriel,' she informed him.

His reply was wary. He was being bombarded by mixed messages himself, none of which he welcomed. 'What about?' he asked, his eyes narrowing.

He breathed an inner sigh of relief when she said, look-

ing around the pristine room, 'I don't dislike anything I've
seen, but I would never have chosen this kind of décor
myself. It's very…impressive and tasteful, but I find it all
very cold and lacking in the comforts I associate with a
home. But you've lived here for years and so you must
like it. In which case, perhaps I'm not the best person to
use for doing the inside of Oakridge House. Maybe you
need someone professional.'

'I have every confidence in you, *querida*.' The endearment, combined with those dark, sexy eyes, did what they
always did. Made her forget what she had been saying.

'To choose stuff *I* would like, Gabriel, which, judging
from what I've seen of your house here, *you* would absolutely hate. And let's face it, Oakridge House *is your*
house, not mine. I don't want to finish my job only to
discover that I haven't done it to your liking.'

'Why don't you leave me to worry about that?' He was
beginning to hate those lines of demarcation that he had
been so keen to establish only a few weeks ago. 'And do
not start rambling on about your duties as my employee,'
he continued repressively.

'I can't just overlook that little technicality,' Laura said
tightly. 'You're paying me a fabulous salary, rescuing me
from penury and I want to repay you by doing a good job.'
God, it was so easy to get carried away on the wings of
day-dreaming, and of reading signals that just weren't
there. Discussing domestic issues was a sure-fire way to
forget exactly what their situation was, and Laura felt compelled to pull herself back from the brink of massive, dangerous self-deception.

'Then as your employer,' he mimicked with thinly
veiled anger, 'who is paying you a fabulous salary and
rescuing you from penury, I order you to furnish the house
precisely how you want to. Use your flair and imagination

and I am happy to leave the outcome up to you.' He turned away and began striding along the corridor, with its plush white carpeting and pale ochre walls.

'There's no need for you to storm off in one of your Latin American moods,' Laura called to him, which instantly made him stop in his tracks and dragged a reluctant smile to his lips. He turned slowly to face her and realised that she had not moved an inch from where she had been standing at the door to the guest room.

'Just as there is no need for you to constantly harp on about your status as my employee.'

They stared at one another from one end of the corridor to the other.

She could have told him that seeing her reduced to that status had been the object of his exercise, and that the only reason he was now choosing to overlook the little detail was because they were lovers and even he must feel some guilt at making love to the woman he had sought out for purposes of revenge.

But she held her tongue.

To have said any of those things would have made their already precarious bubble burst into a million smithereens and she wanted to hold onto the bubble for as long as she could.

Eventually, she shrugged lightly and stepped towards him.

'If you don't mind my taste, then I'll furnish your house just as I would furnish my own,' she said, walking towards him, and she was rewarded with one of those blisteringly sexy smiles that almost made her falter in her tracks.

'I think it is time you saw the master bedroom,' Gabriel murmured, not taking his eyes off her approaching figure for a second. 'It is the one room in the house I actually chose for myself.'

He reached out sideways to push open a door to his right, watching her intently as she came towards him and only turning away when she too turned to gape at the room in front of her.

Gone was the impersonal beauty of the previous rooms she had explored. Here was a room that breathed masculinity. The bed was very low to the ground and the dark, swirling colours of the quilt demanded touching. A rich, dark wooden chest of drawers banked one wall and the pale carpet was almost unseen beneath a massive Persian rug that dominated the floor space. Heavy, deep blue velvet drapes completed the feeling of eroticism.

'You like it?' he whispered into her ear and all Laura could do was nod in wonder at the vibrant mix of colours, none of which seemed out of place although most of them clashed.

'The quilt cover is silk,' he said softly. 'It feels magnificent against bare skin. Would you like to try?'

The mere thought of them writhing naked on top of the silk made her skin begin to tingle, and with supreme confidence he took her hand and led her over to the bed, leaving her to stand by it only for as long as it took him to draw the curtains, plunging the room into instant darkness.

'A sensual boudoir,' Laura said as he lit four bulky candles of varying heights on the chest of drawers. 'Was this your intention when you…created it?'

Gabriel nodded and omitted to mention that it had been a chaste boudoir. He had never brought any of his women back to this house, preferring to see them in his penthouse in London. She was the first, but damned if she would know that.

He moved to where she was still standing and pulled off the shirt, groaning involuntarily as his hands slipped under the vest to find the heavy warmth of her bare breasts.

He rolled his thumbs over the tightened peaks of her nipples and half closed his eyes as she slipped the vest over her head and tossed it to the ground. Then the trousers. Down they came, followed by the lacy underwear. She had been right. Making love in a car did not lend itself to the delight of seeing her exquisite, naked body.

'And what would you like me to do on this silk duvet of yours?' Laura murmured seductively.

'For starters, just lie on it and let me see you.'

It felt as beautiful as it had promised. Laura stretched on the bed, watching him through half-closed eyes, and began moving sensuously for his languid viewing. When her hand trailed along her stomach to ruffle the fine fair hair that guarded her sex, Gabriel sank onto the covers with a grunt of savage passion and captured her wandering hand with his own.

'You little hussy,' he growled. 'Do not even think about touching yourself. That is for my enjoyment only.'

And he was about to prove that very point when the doorbell shrieked into the thick silence and Anna's voice crackled on the intercom in the bedroom, laughing and asking Gabriel, 'Where are you?'

CHAPTER NINE

LAURA walked tentatively towards the kitchen. The sound of Anna's voice had galvanised them both into action. In Gabriel's case, it had been a simple matter of running his fingers through his hair whilst swearing darkly under his breath about interruptions, and then going downstairs to open the front door.

In Laura's case, she had slipped back on her clothes with the nervous tension of a teenager being caught on the couch with her boyfriend when her parents should have been safely out. It was ridiculous, she told herself severely. They were both consenting adults. Which just went to bring home to her in all its ugly clarity the clandestine nature of their relationship. They were fine romping around in the sack just so long as reality didn't manage to break through.

She peeped into the kitchen to find that Gabriel was nowhere to be seen, although Anna was sitting comfortably at the kitchen table, quietly composed with her fingers linked on the glass surface.

'This is a ridiculous table to have in a kitchen, wouldn't you agree?' The dark-haired woman smiled and Laura relaxed and walked in. 'I told Gabriel to get rid of it years ago, and, in all fairness, he agreed every time I mentioned it, but, like all men, did nothing about the advice.'

'Hi.' Laura smiled back cautiously. 'I'm sorry. We weren't…expecting you…but it's lovely to see you again.' She hovered, not too sure what to say. Anna was right. Kitchens should be comfortable and chrome and glass did not constitute comfort, but it would have been ludicrous to embark on a conversation about a kitchen table. 'Where…where is Gabriel?'

'I sent him out.'

'You sent him out?'

'To get some oil for my car,' Anna explained. 'The little red light started appearing on my way here and, being a woman, I have no idea how to put oil in.' She shrugged and gave Laura a conspiratorial smile that suggested she was more than adept at putting oil in her car. 'Besides, I wanted to talk to you without my cousin glowering in the background. Shall we have some coffee?' She stood up and headed towards the cappuccino maker and began operating it in a professional manner, fetching coffee from one of the cupboards and mugs from a drawer.

'You drove here to talk to me?' Laura asked in bewilderment. 'What about?'

'How do you take your coffee?'

'White, no sugar. Thank you.' Laura sat down and tilted her chair so that she could look at what Anna was doing.

'I needed to see Gabriel, actually. In fact, I telephoned the house, but you must have just left. The foreman there told me that you were heading down here. Apparently Gabriel had said that he was to lock up behind him because they were going to Berkshire and might not be back in time before they were due to leave. Naturally, I assumed that you would be coming here and I thought I would kill two birds with one stone. Discuss some business with Gabriel and also grab some time with you. Here you go, coffee almost as you would get it in a restaurant. Without the grated chocolate on top.' Without giving Laura time to ponder the little issue of why Gabriel's cousin wanted to talk to *her*, she rested the mug on the table and sat down.

She looked as stunning as she had done the first time

Laura had set eyes on her. Her brown hair was neatly tied back, though this time in a more casual French braid, to suit her more casual outfit of pale brown cord trousers, flat brogues and a cream, thin jersey top with a fine ribbed pattern running vertically down.

'So. How is the house coming along?'

'That's what you wanted to discuss?' Laura breathed a sigh of relief. 'Well, Gabriel suggested that we do the easy bits first, so at the moment I'm working on updating the house.' She grimaced and then smiled. 'Nothing has been done on it for as long as I can remember. All the wallpaper is being stripped and a lot of the furniture will be replaced. I shall keep a few of the old pieces that belonged to Mum and Dad and then sell the rest, although a lot of it will fetch token amounts. There's very little market for second-hand furniture these days.'

'And how do you feel about it? You know, working and renovating a house that used to belong to you?' Anna sipped some of her coffee whilst looking at Laura levelly over the rim of the mug.

'I look on the bright side. That things could have been a lot worse for me. At least I have a roof over my head and, when my job at the stables is over, I should have saved sufficient money to get a small place of my own.' Why did she get the feeling that they were skirting around an issue? Nibbling the appetiser in preparation for the main meal? And why did she get the feeling that the main meal was not going to be to her liking?

'And Gabriel has moved in, I gather?'

Laura flushed and drank some of her coffee. 'He said he wanted to be on hand so that he could have input into what was going on. He said that it would have been difficult to travel up when he was needed from London and that it was easier to communicate with his office via computer.' She half expected Anna to give a snort of laughter at that, but was disconcerted to find that she just continued looking thoughtfully at her, as if weighing up something in her mind.

'And you two…have become close, have you?'

Laura felt a brief flare of anger at the intrusiveness of the question, but it was immediately quenched by the gentle look in the other woman's eyes.

'I don't mean to be nosy,' Anna apologised. 'But Gabriel did explain a bit of the relationship between the two of you…that you used to know each other a long time ago…'

'I was still a teenager at the time. Gabriel came to the stables occasionally.'

'My cousin is a very passionate man, Laura…' Anna looked a little embarrassed at this observation but she drew in a deep breath and continued anyway. 'Under any other circumstances, I would leave him to get on with his life, but I like you and I disapprove of his tactics.'

'His tactics?' So here it was. The starter course was finished and they were on to the main meal and Laura knew exactly where it was heading.

'He rescued you from your situation so that he could avenge himself of what he saw as an insult delivered many years ago…' She paused and looked at Laura with blazing honesty. 'He can be a very persuasive man, full of charm. Too much charm, really, and I am only cautioning you against falling in love with him because he will hurt you.'

Too late for that little warning, Laura thought restlessly to herself, not that it would have helped anyway. She had never fallen out of love with him.

'I know you think that I am being intrusive, poking my nose in matters that do not concern me, but…' she sought around for a tactful way to say what she wanted to say

'…you strike me as a gentle, maybe emotionally vulnerable girl, even after all you have been through…'

Laura counteracted this accurate observation by gulping down some coffee and then staring fixedly at the pattern on her mug before reluctantly raising her eyes to meet Anna's.

'I can take care of myself.'

'Even when it comes to Gabriel?' She sighed. 'I gather that he is getting you out of his system and, in so doing, it would be easy for you to absorb him into yours and he will…he will never marry you.'

There. The finality of her words hung in the air between them and Laura drew her shoulders up.

'I'm not a fool. I know that. So it's just as well that I haven't made the mistake of falling in love with him, isn't it?'

'Isn't it just.' Gabriel's voice from the kitchen doorway exploded like a bomb in the kitchen and he walked towards them, his angled face devoid of expression. His hands were thrust into his trouser pockets and he didn't even dare look at Laura because to look at her would have been to be consumed with rage.

Had he expected anything else from her? He had wooed and seduced a woman who felt nothing for him but lust and all his plans for revenge lay in ruins around his feet because, fool that he was, he had actually committed the same cardinal sin he had committed years before. He had misread her signals and allowed himself to be lulled into loving her all over again.

He didn't know who filled him with more rage. Her or himself.

'Because Anna is absolutely right.' He stopped directly in front of Laura and steeled himself to meet her brown, dismayed eyes. 'I will never marry you.' Then he turned to his cousin with a hard expression. 'And you were totally out of order in coming here so that you could interfere in matters that do not concern you. Running around behind my back and stirring up trouble is not part of your job specification.'

'I could not live with my conscience if I had said nothing, Gabriel.'

'Which is hardly my problem. Now I think it is time you left.'

'I need to talk to you about a couple of our clients.'

'Not now.'

Anna stood up and glared accusingly at her cousin. In all fairness, Laura thought, she did not appear in the least intimidated.

'I'll leave,' Laura suggested, clearing her throat and standing up. She had slept with this man, loving him and knowing that he did not return her love, knowing that he was playing with her, but she had managed to justify her responses to herself because neither of them had crossed the dangerous barrier of discussing their emotions and what they felt or didn't feel. Now, though, with everything spilled out into the open, turning a blind eye to reality was no longer an option.

'Leave and go where?' Gabriel asked coldly and she flinched at the expression in his eyes.

'Back to Oakridge.'

'And how do you imagine you will get there?' he asked icily. 'Sprout wings and fly?' He knew that she was desperate to retreat and that whatever they'd had between them was well and truly over. He could read it in her brown eyes, which could barely meet his without sliding away. *So it's over*, he thought. Well, it was inevitable. But he felt as if a light was being turned off inside him. Light or not, though, he would not ask her back into his bed.

'I could wait and perhaps, Anna, you could give me a lift to the nearest station when you're leaving?'

'She will do no such thing. She is leaving right now and you will stay as planned.'

'Gabriel, let her go.'

'Goodbye, Anna. You know where the front door is. Feel free to use it. You can telephone me in the morning to discuss whatever business you wanted to discuss.' He didn't even bother glancing at his cousin when he said this. He just continued pinning Laura with his eyes into frozen immobility.

She felt rather than saw the other woman reluctantly leave the kitchen, but, instead of feeling relieved that at least one member in the cast of this awful, unfolding drama was out of the way, she was overcome with sudden, wild tension that made her legs shake, and she collapsed back onto the kitchen chair.

'You look nervous,' Gabriel said into the tautly stretching silence and he forced himself to offer her a mimicry of a smile. 'I have no idea why. You surely must have known all along that what we had was not going to go anywhere.'

'Of course I knew that, Gabriel.'

'So why do you look so shell-shocked? Nothing my cousin said should have disturbed you.' He hated himself for his reluctance to let her go. With controlled calmness, he walked across to a cupboard, extracted a bottle and proceeded to help himself to a generous serving of whisky, to which he added a couple of blocks of ice, but nothing else. He needed it. In fact, he had never needed a drink as much as he now needed this one. The stark realisation of how he felt about the woman sitting in muted silence only feet away from him had struck him where he hurt most.

At the very core of his masculine pride and at the heart of his formidable self-control.

'And don't think that you can start bleating on about being used.' He swigged back a mouthful of the drink. 'You threw yourself willingly at me.'

'I wasn't about to start bleating on about anything.'

'Then why the strained expression? I told you myself once that you meant nothing to me.' Just saying it made him feel a bastard but, in some crazy way, punishing her was to punish himself and it was something he was compelled to do.

'I know, but...'

He felt a flare of treacherous hope and squashed it ruthlessly. 'But you thought that you could change my mind? Is that it?' he taunted. 'Did you imagine that I would get so enraptured with your warm, available body that I would begin to hear the distant sound of wedding bells?'

'You sound as if you hate me, Gabriel,' Laura whispered. 'How could you have made love to me if you had hated me?'

'You flatter yourself. Hate is a big emotion.' He gave an expressive shrug of his big shoulders. 'We had an arrangement by mutual consent in which emotion did not play a part.'

'I think it's time I left.' She hoped that she would find the control of her legs that she needed and was relieved when they did not sink from under her as she rose to her feet and walked woodenly towards the kitchen door, skirting around so that she did not come within touching distance of him. 'I'll walk to the station if you're not prepared to drop me. Or I can get a taxi. Would you mind if I use your phone?'

'I take it that you do not wish to continue our lovemaking, which was so rudely interrupted an hour ago?'

Gabriel felt that his heart were being physically wrenched out of his chest.

'I think it's best if we stick to what we should have stuck to from the start,' Laura said, pausing to look at him, loving every ounce of the proud, cruel man standing across the kitchen from her. 'Business. If, that is, you still want me to work for you at the stables.'

'Why should that have changed?' He deposited his glass on the counter and then leaned against it, propping himself up by his hands. 'Of course, it might be a little awkward, in view of our new-found business-only relationship, if I were to carry on working at the house, so I will have my things collected some time tomorrow.'

He was letting her go without a backward glance, Laura thought in anguish, and, amidst all her emotions, at least surprise wasn't one of them. He had never lied to her. She was the one who had been guilty of lying to herself.

'And I shall drop you to the station myself. Never let it be said that I am not the perfect...' his mouth twisted cynically '...gentleman.'

The short ten-minute drive to the station was completed in total silence and he stopped the car only to allow her time to get out, not even killing the engine to imply that he might stick around if even to see that she got safely on a train back to the house.

The only words he spoke were to inform her that he expected to be kept advised of what was going on with the decorating of the house and that all major decisions were naturally to be referred to him, as her boss.

'Naturally,' Laura responded with equal cool and she held her head high as she walked away from him, only allowing her emotions to spill over when she was on the train heading back.

At least he would no longer be working under the same

roof and she would be spared having to live alongside him, without the joy of knowing his body at night. How easy it had been for her to ignore the truth and kid herself that it didn't really exist.

Anna had simply forced a situation and she should have been grateful for that because love just grew with time and her love would have known no boundaries.

It was late by the time she reached the house. The workmen had all left, thankfully, although the house hardly felt like a home with the wallpaper stripped from a lot of the walls and the downstairs carpet in the process of being removed.

Laura was barely aware of the chaos, however. She bypassed the kitchen, ignoring the rumbling in her stomach, and headed straight for the bedroom. Luxuriating in a bath seemed like a needless waste of time, so she had a quick shower instead, and then got into her pyjamas, which were items of clothing that she had not recently been wearing.

Gabriel had told her that he had liked to feel her nakedness next to him even when he was asleep, and she had been all too happy to oblige. Now they were a mocking reminder that all of that was over. She was back to pyjamas and loneliness with the added bonus of a future filled with anguished memories and regret.

Gabriel, she was sure, was not lying in his king-sized bed with its silk duvet, nursing thoughts of misery and loss. Hopefully, he was not flicking through his little black book and seeking out her immediate replacement. No, she more imagined him sitting in front of a computer somewhere in the house, in another of those designer-clad, soulless rooms, working.

He would have been. He should have been. If only he could manage to stand up without falling over. Alcohol never had been his way of dealing with anything but, from the relative comfort of a chair in one of the sitting areas, it seemed like a damned good idea. It blurred his feverish, maddening thoughts into a manageable numbness. Unfortunate that it also had such a numbing effect on his limbs, aside, that was, from his arm, which seemed to function perfectly when it came to topping up the whisky glass.

All he needed now was to fall asleep and be spared the occasional pain when a coherent thought managed to find its way to his brain, to remind him of what he had lost and to jeer at him for having got himself in such a position that he had been vulnerable enough to feel the pain of losing.

She didn't love him. Never had, never would. She had just enjoyed the sex he had provided. He had heard it with his own two ears, and, drunk or not, he was not so far gone that he couldn't remember that much. He had preached to her a load of bull that it shouldn't have made a scrap of difference, but he could have been preaching to himself because it did. He could never touch her again now that he knew, for sure, how emotionally indifferent she was to him, but he couldn't imagine a world in which she was not there to touch and talk to and laugh with. He shook his head in a dazed fashion and wondered whether another small drink might not send him into the arms of sweet, forgetful sleep. Unfortunately, the bottle, he realised, was empty, and he was too damned heavy-limbed to do anything about replacing it.

At a little past midnight, he finally drifted to sleep with the grim realisation that morning was not going to bring a whole lot more peace of mind.

But he would never go back to her. Even if being apart from her killed him in the process. He would have his things removed and keep in casual touch via telephone, or better still e-mail, even if that meant buying her a computer and getting someone to have it up and running. If he had to come face to face with her, he would bring someone in tow, preferably a very sexy woman, just to prove once and for all how little she had meant to him and to safeguard himself from doing something he might later regret. Such as fall back under her spell.

In a confused way, it all seemed to make sense when the alcohol was still swimming through his bloodstream, and in the morning, when he finally surfaced, he had enough wit to get on the phone and order his secretary to arrange for his things to be returned to London.

Which was why, soon after three in the afternoon, Laura was at hand to witness the quick and efficient departure of all evidence that Gabriel had ever set up office in the house.

She watched as every electronic item was carefully dismantled and boxed, and then signed the relevant sheet with an unsteady hand.

Then she sat at the now-empty dining table with her chin propped up in the palm of her hand and allowed her mind to drift away on its own unhappy course.

Only the sound of the telephone ringing brought her back to life, and when she heard Anna's voice down the line she almost wept at the vague contact with the man she loved.

'I'm phoning to say how sorry I am for...not minding my own business,' Anna said anxiously. 'I had no idea how deep in you both were. And I certainly never expected that Gabriel would sneak up on us the way he did.'

'I'm not in deep,' Laura denied weakly. 'So we slept together, but we're adults. It's not unheard of, you know, sex between two consenting adults who are attracted to one another, even though there's no emotional commitment. It doesn't mean...it doesn't mean that...' She couldn't complete the rest of her empty protest.

'Oh, but it does. I could see for myself, Laura.'

'I... Oh, why am I lying? What's the use? I was always in love with him, but everything comes to an end and there's no need to apologise, Anna. You did what you thought was the right thing to do and...*both*? We weren't *both* deep in anything. *I* was deep in, but you heard Gabriel yourself and I can't even say that he strung me along because he didn't. I think a part of me was just always waiting for him to come back, so that I could pick up where we left off, unconditionally.'

'So now you are back at the riding stables and he has remained at that gruesome mausoleum of his in Berkshire, am I correct?'

'You're correct.'

'And presumably the fool has had all his things removed from the house?'

'They've just taken away his fax machine, his computer, all the office equipment...'

'And you let them?'

'Of course I let them!' Laura said robustly. 'What else was I supposed to do? Fling my arms across the door and refuse them entry to a house that doesn't even belong to me? Two strapping men?'

'And you have not considered fighting for Gabriel?'

'Fighting how?' Laura wailed. 'He doesn't want me!'

'If Gabriel did not want you, he would never have returned in the first place. He would have read about the stables, had a chuckle and moved on to the next page. If he did not want you, his eyes would not have burned with anger when he realised that you wanted to leave his house with me. Gabriel is a blind idiot and one day, when all this is over, I am going to get him to grovel at my feet in gratitude for being the interfering old bag that I am!' And she sounded so spirited and so convincing that foolish thoughts began to multiply in Laura's head and she seized the thread of hope they promised with both hands, rushing to get her diary when Anna suggested that they meet up and chat.

She flicked through the pages, then flicked back through them and a little cold film of perspiration broke out all over her at what she was seeing for the first time.

Her period. Where was it? For years she had adhered to her mother's guidelines about always writing the commencement of her period in her diary because *a woman could not afford not to be tuned into her reproductive system*. But they had been very careful. From the very first, he had taken the necessary precautions. Well…not from the *very first*, Laura thought slowly. No, that first time had been when they had gone riding and she had surrendered. Which had been…a few weeks ago.

But she had had no symptoms. No sickness, no tiredness, no increased appetite. Nothing.

'Hello? Are you still there?'

'Yes,' Laura said faintly. 'Look, someone has just banged at the front door. Can I get back to you with a date? I'd love to meet up.'

Her heart was pounding when she replaced the receiver, although when she told the foreman that she was just stepping out for half an hour or so her voice sounded perfectly normal.

Stepping out to go to the nearest pharmacy, even though she knew in her gut that the trip was unnecessary. Unless her reproductive system had decided to go on a short holiday to cope with all the recent emotional turmoil, she was pregnant.

Nevertheless when, a little over an hour later, she saw

two clear blue lines appear in the two windows of the device that boasted a ninety-nine per-cent accuracy rate, Laura gave a little moan of shock.

So what happened next?

What happens, a little voice in her head said, is you pick up that telephone and you arrange to meet Gabriel. No point waiting for him to call at some point in time, because that point in time was never going to arrive. Gabriel's pride was as big as a mountain. He would never come back to her, and, despite what Anna had said, she really didn't know *what* his feelings towards her were. Yes, he wanted her, or at least he had done. And he was not as indifferent emotionally to her as he pretended to be. That, at any rate, was what she was going to have to believe when she picked that phone up in five minutes' time.

He wasn't in. Big anticlimax. But his secretary must have detected the urgency in her voice because she gave Laura his mobile phone number.

This time he did answer and in a voice that left Laura in no doubt that, whatever he was doing, he was not going to have the time to listen to what she had to say.

'You need to cultivate a better telephone manner,' were her first nervous words and she punctuated the observation with shaky laughter.

Hearing her voice was so unexpected that it took Gabriel a few seconds before he realised that he was talking to the woman who had plagued his thoughts the night before. He had missed a breakfast meeting because he had just not been able to get out of bed in time to make it to the Savoy and he had only just managed to get to his second scheduled meeting for the day, at an impressive smoked-glass building in Canary Wharf.

He abruptly halted his long stride through the offices of DuBarry, obliging the personal assistant who was leading him through to the boardroom to stop as well, and cupped the cell phone in the palm of his hand.

How dared she? How dared she telephone him, *using his mobile phone number no less*, when he was about to go into a very important meeting, after he had made it absolutely clear that he wanted nothing more to do with her? That she could take a running jump off the side of a very steep cliff! Had she no respect for a single word he had spoken?

'What do you want?' God, it was bloody good to hear her voice.

'I hope I'm not interrupting anything.'

'You are, as a matter of fact. Now get to the point, Laura.' He made sure to invest his voice with supreme indifference, overlaid with just the right amount of irritation that would indicate a busy man who had no time for some insignificant ex-lover. He placed his hand over the receiver and whispered to the personal assistant, a ferociously competent-looking woman in her mid-fifties with disciplined hair and a face that would terrify the most hardened of men, that she would have to go ahead of him and explain that he was dealing with a very important call, and would be in as soon as possible.

'I want to talk to you.'

'You have my e-mail address. You will have to learn to make decisions without running to me every two seconds. I thought I had made it perfectly clear to you that you and I are finished and the less contact I have with you, the happier I will be. Now, if that is all...'

Laura gritted her teeth together and clenched her fist. 'I want to see you and it's not about the house.'

'Oh, no? Then what do you want to talk to me about?' He glanced at his watch and realised that he would have to get a move on if he was to complete this meeting in time for his next one. Still. Disgusted though he felt with himself, there was no way he could dismiss her. Just the sound of her voice was sending his system into overdrive.

'I want to talk to you about us,' Laura said bluntly.

'I really have no time for this,' Gabriel said dismissively. 'I am very busy.' The personal assistant reappeared and he glowered at her.

'I don't care how busy you are, Gabriel. I'm not prepared for things between us to end this way.'

'*You* are not prepared?'

'That's right. *I* am not prepared and I shall just keep pestering you until you…meet me.'

'Oh, very well. I will drive up to the house this afternoon. I should be there early evening, but I can warn you now that there will be no point to the meeting.'

Laura was shaking by the time she dropped the receiver back onto its handset. She didn't dare start having doubts about what she had done now that she had done it, but she couldn't help herself. They crept in like pernicious tentacles of ivy and sought to wrap themselves around the fragile little fragments of courage she had tried to instil within herself.

By the time the workmen were leaving the house, she had analysed and re-analysed every nuance of every expression she had ever seen cross his face, searching desperately for signs of hope that he might care about her. She could deal with his pride and his indifference, provided at least some of it was just a veneer, but what if his indifference really did run bone-deep? What if Anna had been utterly wrong?

Eventually, as Laura quickly changed into a pair of jeans and a fresh top she abandoned her pointless train of thoughts and told herself that, at the end of the day, she had no choice but to see him anyway. She was carrying his baby and there was no way she would want to keep him in ignorance of that fact, even if there was a chance that she could have. A father deserved every chance to know of the existence of his child, just as the child would deserve every chance to know of his or her father. Any other route was unthinkable.

She was peering through the side window when Gabriel's car drew up and her heart clenched as he stepped out of the driver's seat and glanced once around him. He had come straight from work. He was still in his suit, although the tie had been removed and the top two buttons of his white shirt were undone. She imagined him restlessly tugging it off as he drove up to the house.

Her courage of earlier on was disappearing at a rate of knots, and by the time she went to the door, where the doorbell was imperiously issuing its summons, it had completely vanished. She literally had no idea what to say as she pulled open the door and was confronted by the harsh, cold expression of two dangerously dark eyes staring at her.

'Gabriel. Hi.'

'You said that you wanted to talk, so here I am. It has been a long trip up through traffic and it will take at least an hour and a half to get back home, so shall we get this talk over and done with as soon as possible?'

Making it clear what his intentions were, Laura thought with plummeting self-confidence. He had come but he was not going to stay the night, whatever she had to say...

CHAPTER TEN

THE kitchen was one of the few rooms as yet untouched by the workforce and Gabriel followed Laura into it, keeping a telling distance and focusing on the bitter pill that he had been forced to swallow and that still stuck in his throat like a bone. What did she want to talk to him about? If she thought that she could wriggle back into his bed and his life, then she was way off target. God, how had he managed to get himself into this hole? The answer, he thought savagely, was quite simple: he had found a spade, dug it and jumped in whilst telling himself that he was totally in control.

His faraway plan to avenge himself for the insult delivered to him seven years previously could not have gone more disastrously wrong. Instead of using her ruthlessly so that he could eventually discard her in his own sweet time, he had caved in once again and the only means he had of extricating himself from the mess was to walk away from it as quickly as his long legs could carry him.

Even looking at her now, the way her body moved like a gazelle in front of him, mesmerised him.

His overriding urge was to close the distance between them, swing her around and make her his.

'Have you eaten?'

She was looking at him, all wide brown eyes and appealing hesitation.

'I am fine. Why don't we just have a cup of coffee and you can tell me what was so important that you felt you had to drag me out here?'

God, but he wasn't making this easy. Laura gritted her teeth together and thought of the little life growing steadily inside her. The thought of tossing that little fact his way made her want to faint.

'Sure, but, if you don't mind, I'll just fix myself something to eat as well.' She knew that he wasn't even looking at her as she busied herself by the counter, making them both a cup of coffee and rustling together the vegetables she had previously chopped and prepared.

The opening remarks she made, about nothing in particular, were met with monosyllabic answers and a tone of disinterest.

This was the behaviour of a man who cared?

Eventually, she turned around, her plate in her hand, and sat facing him at the table.

'So,' Gabriel remarked, finally affording her his attention, 'why don't you just say what you have to say and get it over with, Laura? Instead of the both of us playing this game of polite strangers.'

'Because we're not, are we, Gabriel?'

The directness of her reply took him aback and he narrowed his eyes at her upturned face as she continued to look at him levelly across the table.

'We're lovers.'

'*Were* lovers. You need to get the tense right.'

'What changed, Gabriel? One minute we were on the brink of making love and the next minute you had turned into a raging bull and what we had was gone in a puff of smoke. Was it so meaningless to you?'

A dark flush spread over his high cheekbones. 'If this is going to be a post mortem on a failed relationship, then you are wasting your time.'

'Why? Because you think that I should meekly walk away and accept that I meant nothing to you?'

'I dislike women who cannot face the end of a relationship.' Gabriel shrugged with exaggerated indifference. 'All good things come to an end.' He had won, he thought. He had her in the palm of his hand. That had been his intention. So why was he feeling so damned hollow? Because he had fallen in love with her. Again. Her body was never going to be good enough and he knew that if he allowed her back in, she would wreak further devastation on his heart. But, God, he didn't want to leave this house, this kitchen, *her*.

'Why?'

'Why what?'

'Why do all good things have to come to an end? Are you implying that the only relationship you will ever consider with a woman is one that *isn't* good?'

'Relationships are possible without all the trappings that society forces us to accept.'

'By trappings you mean…what? Love? Marriage?' The last thing she wanted was for this conversation to be reduced to the level of a hypothetical debate, but he just wasn't going to give an inch. If she mentioned the word marriage, he would oblige her by talking about it as an institution, if she mentioned love, he would analyse the meaning of the word and then dismiss it. She shook her head in frustration and rested her forehead lightly on the palm of her hand.

'Have you brought me here so that you can hear me tell you again that I have no intention of ever asking you to marry me?' Gabriel's mouth twisted cynically and she flinched, but held her ground.

'I would never expect you to ask me to marry you, Gabriel,' Laura returned softly.

'Then what?' he grated irritably. He was beginning to

feel uncomfortably hot, and he ran one long brown finger inside the collar of his shirt.

Laura chose to ignore that pointed question. His voice might be callously dismissive and his eyes were as hard as ice, but he was uncomfortable. She could sense it and that gave her failing courage a bit of a boost. She loved this man and she was going to fight for him, and if it didn't work out the way she hoped, then so be it. Better to fight and lose than to walk away and then spend the rest of her life regretting her passivity.

'So if relationships and commitment and marriage isn't about love, Gabriel, what is it all about?'

He shrugged and stood up. He had to. He had to move. The contained energy inside him was killing him.

He restlessly began to prowl through the kitchen, hands shoved aggressively into his pockets, whilst his dark eyes swept over the blonde figure sitting quietly on the chair.

What was she trying to say to him? That she couldn't do without his body? That she was prepared to beg and plead just so that she could get her daily fix of sex? But if sex was what she was after, then why hadn't she greeted him at the door in the clothes of seduction? Small, revealing and provocative?

'Who knows?' he answered ambiguously. 'Maybe the best relationship is one based on business.'

'I thought that that was precisely what we had,' Laura replied drily.

'Not quite the sort of business I had in mind,' Gabriel said smoothly. 'I meant business that involves a two-way profit.' He picked up a small flowerpot resting on the counter, in which a clump of basil was struggling to grow, and inspected it in some detail before putting it down.

'Gabriel, sit down. I can't concentrate when you're

stalking through this kitchen like a cat burglar on the look-
out for the family heirlooms.'

'What is there to concentrate on?' He felt a fierce tug
of excitement and fought it tooth and nail.

'I don't want what we have to end,' Laura began, drawing in a deep breath and watching as Gabriel pushed back
his chair and proceeded to inspect her through half-closed
eyes. 'And before you open your mouth to speak, let me
just finish.'

He could have told her that the last thing he was going
to do was open his mouth. Behind the scowling façade, he
was hanging onto her every word.

'Seven years ago, you walked away and I let you. I let
you because I was young and marriage was something that
I had never, ever even contemplated. Maybe my parents
had something to do with it, I don't know. But I was a
fool.'

'Especially when you look at me now,' Gabriel intoned
grimly.

'That has nothing to do with it,' Laura told him impa-
tiently. 'I don't care whether you made a million or not.
What I care about is that you...came back. And I know
why you came back...' All of this was hard and it took
every ounce of courage she possessed to lay every card on
the table, but this part was the hardest. Acknowledging the
cold, ugly truth that had brought him to her aid. She could
feel a lump of self-pity gather at the back of her throat and
she choked it down.

'You came back,' she continued in a whispered mono-
tone, 'because you wanted revenge and what better revenge than to have me in a position of indebtedness to
you. The shoe was on the other foot, as far as you were
concerned, and you could have the last laugh. But what
matters to me is that you came back. I realised that I loved

you then and I never stopped loving you.' She glared at him, daring him to sneer at the admission that had drained her, but he didn't. He looked lost for words.

'You expect me to believe that? I heard you tell Anna just the opposite, *querida*.' He didn't dare give way, but his heart was soaring like a bird. He wanted to jump up, sing, wrap his arms around her, all at the same time.

'When?'

'When? What do you mean *when*? Yesterday, of course. When the two of you were having your cosy chat in my kitchen.'

'I spoke to Anna this morning and told her everything. Well, almost everything.' Laura sighed and ran her fingers through her hair. She was perspiring, as if she had run a marathon, and her hands were shaking. 'I told her how I felt about you. I can't change how you feel, whether you believe me or not, but...' she met his eyes steadily, without blinking '...I love you, Gabriel Greppi, and I wouldn't be able to live with myself if this all fizzled out and you never knew how I really felt. When I told Anna that I wasn't involved with you, I was lying. It's as simple as that. I had a moment of pride. I might have thought that you...would have recognised the passing weakness.' She paused long enough for the silence to settle, and then said shakily, 'Aren't you going to say anything? Even if all you have to say is that you don't believe a word I'm saying?'

'I cannot ask you to marry me...I asked you once...' *A moment of pride!* He had a lifetime of pride. He couldn't ask her to marry him, not again, even though he believed every word she had just spoken. The truth of it was shining in her eyes. But his pride.

'Is that all you have to say, Gabriel?' Laura stood up. 'Nothing else? You damned, stubborn...okay, you win. I've told you how I feel and if you have nothing to say, then you were right, it's over.' She had gambled everything. What price one more gamble?

His head shot up and he stood up as well, moving swiftly over to her.

'I…'

'Marry me.' Laura looked at him with blazing challenge. 'What we have is good, very good, and it'll get better. Take a chance.'

'You're asking me to marry you?' His face darkened and he dropped his head.

'That's right. Marry me.'

'Or else what?'

'Or else you'll regret giving up the greatest love you will ever know.' She tentatively placed her hand on the side of his face and caressed his skin.

'No,' he murmured hoarsely.

So this was it. She had taken the gamble and lost.

'Right,' Laura said hollowly.

'I mean, no, I would not just regret giving up the greatest love I will ever know…I would regret a great deal more than that…' He tilted her chin so that she was looking at him and what she read on his face, the tenderness and love, made the breath catch in her throat. 'I lost the only thing worth having the day I walked out of your life, my darling.' He buried his head into her neck and then, when he had gathered his self-control, that priceless commodity that had been in very short supply ever since he had gone barging back into her life, he raised his head once again to catch her eyes with his.

'I came back, yes, for the lowest of reasons. I thought I was over you and that I was simply closing a chapter. God help me, I saw myself as the all-powerful one who had returned to settle old scores. But the fact is, there were no scores to settle. I should never have let my pride kill our relationship then. I should have listened to what you were saying because every word you said was right. We were both young. We could have waited a little longer, grown to know each other better, but I was having none of it. When I think that this cursed pride of mine would have caused my own destruction a second time, my blood runs cold.'

'You love me,' Laura said with a wondering smile.

'I adore you. When you called me on my mobile this morning and told me that you wanted to see me, to talk, I couldn't wait for my meetings to be over. I couldn't wait to be in your presence again because it's only when you are around that I feel alive.'

'And you'll marry me?'

'You don't intend to let me wriggle away again, do you, *querida*?' This time he gave a low, velvety chuckle that made her go to liquid inside.

'That's certainly one of the reasons.'

'One of the reasons?'

'Would you mind if we sat down? I feel as if my legs are going to buckle from under me.'

Thank goodness the kitchen stools were generously built. Big enough for Gabriel to comfortably sit with Laura on his lap. She rested her head on his shoulder and realised, suddenly, that the full extent of his love was about to take a serious knock. Marriage, passion and a three-year honeymoon spelled a different story from marriage, a swelling stomach and midnight feeds.

'Better?' he murmured into her ear. 'Perhaps we should go upstairs, lie down on the bed. Altogether more satisfactory for what I have in mind, now that I have been browbeaten into marrying you, you beautiful witch.'

'Okay, but first there's something else I have to tell you.' She sat up and looked him straight in the eye. What she saw was a tiny, black-eyed infant with a mop of curly dark hair and a gummy smile. 'If we get married, it might be an idea for it to be sooner rather than later.'

Comprehension took a matter of seconds. She could see it dawning in his eyes and then he grinned with radiant, unchecked joy. 'You are pregnant?'

'I did the test this morning. I...it happened the first time we made love, when we didn't use any protection. If you don't want to marry me now that you know, then I'll understand. It's a big responsibility and it's just been dropped on your lap like a bombshell.'

'Not want to marry you?' He placed his hand on her stomach, still flat and toned. 'There is no way I would *not* marry you, and the fact that you are pregnant with my child, *our* child, is the icing on the cake.' He stroked her stomach in slow circles and Laura's breathing quickened, a little fact that did not escape his notice.

'Perhaps we *should* go upstairs,' she murmured, catching the satisfied expression on his face and blushing.

'Oh, yes? And what did you have in mind when we get there?'

'You know exactly what I have in mind!' She led him up the stairs, holding his hand, and only paused to look at him when they were on the threshold of the bedroom. 'I shall lose my figure,' she warned him and he nodded.

'So perhaps I ought to explore you thoroughly now, mmm? Before our baby starts pushing out your stomach and making those breasts of yours heavy and big with milk? I find the thought of you pregnant very erotic, as a matter of fact...'

And he then proceeded to show her how erotic he found her. But nothing could be as erotic as the thought that at long last the dream of happiness had become reality and that from here onwards their steps forward would be taken together...for ever.

EPILOGUE

'GABRIEL, darling…' It was three-seventeen in the morning. Laura could glimpse the illuminated hands of the clock on the table next to her beloved husband, whose naked body was warm next to hers. She brushed her lips against his cheek and then grimaced as another contraction hardened her stomach.

Nearly two weeks overdue and a girl, Gabriel was forever telling her with a grin, because only a female would keep everyone waiting for as long as she had done.

'Gabriel, don't panic, but…'

It must have been the word *panic* that did it because his eyes flicked open and the first words he uttered were a heartfelt, *'Dios!'*

'I'm only just beginning,' Laura said soothingly, gritting her teeth together as another contraction ripped through her, and watching with amusement as Gabriel leapt out of the bed and began flinging on his clothes, only switching the light on as an afterthought.

'Laura, my sweetest, God, you are in pain.'

'It happens around this time of the pregnancy.' She began edging herself off the bed and he raced to her side, half tripping over his trousers, which were not fully on.

'You're wincing. You're trying to be brave but you're wincing. I am not blind! I can see!'

'Calm down.'

'How can I calm down? Your bag. I'll get your bag. Where *is* your bag? Of course I know where your bag is! Stay calm, Laura, don't panic!'

He had solicitously helped her pack her bag over a month ago, insisting on adding so many unlisted items to the contents that in the end she had warned him that he might have to buy a trunk to hold it all.

'I'm not...'

'And do not get dressed!' he ordered from their *en suite* dressing room, from which he was fetching the bag as well as jumpers and coats for them both. 'I will help you!'

'I think I can manage.' Sometimes she wondered why she bothered to say certain things when she could always so accurately predict his responses. As she expected, he completed the job of getting her nightdress off, his voice laced with frantic panic as he demanded to know whether she was up to changing or whether they should just fling a coat over her and hurry to the hospital. Maybe, he fulminated, they should take the helicopter.

'I don't think the hospital has anywhere for helicopters to land,' Laura said lovingly.

'I'll carry you to the car.'

'I can walk, you idiot. Just support me a little.'

Seven months of wedded bliss and she was still awe-struck at the love that could so easily have eluded her, a love that seemed to grow with each passing minute. Their wedding had been simple and attended only by his closest family members and their mutual friends and she had enjoyed every second of it, basking in his tenderness and adoration, which he made no attempt to hide.

She could sense his frustration as he navigated the dark lanes, and finally the wider, better-lit roads, that he couldn't take the pain away from her. By the time they reached the hospital, he was far more jittery than she was and she had to murmur softly that there was no need to worry, that everything was perfectly straightforward and, really, the staff there knew how to deal with women in labour.

'How can you be so calm?' he accused, seething with annoyance at the seemingly languid manner in which they were checked in whilst he tapped his foot and glowered.

'One of us has to be.'

'I am calm.'

'Oh, yes, as calm as someone on the verge of a nervous breakdown.' Their eyes met and Gabriel felt his heart swell with love, then finally things started happening. They were shown to the labour ward and after a brief examination, from which he was excluded by some very decisive drawing of curtains around the bed, the next few hours raced by with the terrifying speed of a runaway train.

And there was nothing he could do! Only be with the woman he loved, hold her hand, mop her brow and try to remember all those pearls of wisdom he had read in the various pregnancy books he had devoured, much to his wife's amusement, and most of which he had now comprehensively forgotten.

'She's doing fine, Mr Greppi,' one of the two midwives told him at some point in the proceedings, 'but you look as though you could use a cup of tea. She'll be here for at least another couple of hours. Why don't you go down to the canteen and have something hot to drink?'

'I'm here for the duration.'

'Well, just don't go fainting on me.'

'I never faint. Shouldn't there be a consultant in here?'

'I've delivered more babies than you've had hot dinners, young man.' But the middle-aged woman grinned and winked at him. 'She'll be fine.'

Never in his life had Gabriel felt more racked with nerves and never in his life had he ever been so reduced to speechless awe than when, an hour and a half later, he glimpsed his baby as one final push expelled his son. Eight pounds, eleven ounces and groggily unaware of his surroundings until he drew in his breath and released an outraged shriek.

'It's a baby boy,' the midwife said, bustling with him and then handing him wrapped in a blanket to Laura. 'What a lot of hair.'

Laura looked down at the small bundle lying against her, fists closed and eyelids fluttering, and smiled.

'We have a son.' Pride and joy threatened to make his eyes water. 'Didn't I tell you that it would be a boy?' He stroked Laura's blonde hair away from her face, which was still glistening with perspiration, and she glanced up at him with a tender smile.

'Did you?'

'Of course I did,' Gabriel said gruffly. 'And look at that mop of black hair. He looks just like his father.' He bent to kiss his wife and then the small, warm cheek of his baby and watched in fascination as the little bundle wriggled and stretched and then settled back into position.

'My family,' he said with a lump in his throat. 'My perfect family.'